HAPPILY EVER HIS

MOVIE STARS IN MARYLAND, BOOK ONE

DELANCEY STEWART

Copyright © 2019 by Delancey Stewart

All rights reserved.

No part of this book may be reproduced in any form or by any electronic or mechanical means, including information storage and retrieval systems, without written permission from the author, except for the use of brief quotations in a book review.

CONTENTS

Prologue	1
Chapter One	3
Chapter Two	7
Chapter Three	17
Chapter Four	25
Chapter Five	40
Chapter Six	51
Chapter Seven	61
Chapter Eight	74
Chapter Nine	91
Chapter Ten	97
Chapter Eleven	103
Chapter Twelve	119
Chapter Thirteen	127
Chapter Fourteen	135
Chapter Fifteen	144
Chapter Sixteen	153
Chapter Seventeen	158
Chapter Eighteen	164
Chapter Nineteen	172
Chapter Twenty	185
Chapter Twenty-One	193
Chapter Twenty-Two	200
Chapter Twenty-Three	202
Chapter Twenty-Four	205
Chapter Twenty-Five	212
Epilogue	220
Also by Delancey Stewart	229

PROLOGUE
RYAN

I'll say this here because it's important.
I'm not the kind of guy who believes in fairy tales. Or happy endings, unless they're in the movies. That's just not the way my life has gone.

I'm the action hero, the guy who takes the role and does his own stunts, the hard-working actor who just hasn't quite managed to get his star to stick. But I'm working on it. Because honestly? I need the money.

Of course, most of the public remembers me for my role in an epic television drama called *Charade of Stones*. And after the writers wrecked the whole series in one fiery ending episode full of rampaging elephants and flying monkeys? Well, I was still getting questions about that.

Flying monkeys, for fuck's sake.

But actors don't write the shows. You know that right?

I was scrapping to make it in Hollywood, doing whatever it took. That's why I never thought I'd find the role I'd been made for so far away from the Sunset Strip. And I never thought real life would be the most important role I'd ever play.

And I definitely never believed in love at first sight.
Until I saw Tess Manchester.

CHAPTER ONE
RYAN

A voice rang out as I stepped into the terminal at LAX with my arm wrapped around the waist of America's most famous movie star. "How long have you two been seeing each other, Ryan?"

Here we went.

Juliet Manchester pressed herself against my chest, her arms around me lightly, turning to me to smile up into my face and laugh as if she didn't have a care in the world. At this moment, I was Mr. It. I was the guy almost every red-blooded American man wanted to be. And maybe the only guy who didn't care much about being here. I was doing this because I was supposed to. It was a job.

"Juliet! Juliet!" The assembled reporters and photographers called out to us as we turned and made our way through the terminal.

Juliet's hand snaked down to my butt and she pulled me to a stop again, her other hand coming to my chest. She looked up at me, blinking the big green eyes and turning up her pert little nose, her lips in a pout.

Man, she was good at this.

I glanced around at the cameras, and angled my head in for a kiss.

Hell, that was why I was here, after all. I met her lips with mine as flashes lit the terminal area. Our carry-on bags made the embrace awkward, but I did the best I could to make it authentic. Juliet played her part too, her hand gripping my butt as she pushed herself into me. It probably looked pretty hot. I hoped it did at least. We were actors, weren't we?

I mean, I was a struggling actor maybe, but I hoped that said less about my talent and more about my opportunities so far. And this right here? This was an opportunity. I needed to maximize it, no matter how wrong it might feel on a human level.

I hoisted my bag to my shoulder, freeing my arm, pulled her small frame closer to me and moved my lips softly against hers, deepening the kiss after a moment. When her tongue met mine, I braced myself for the explosive sparks I was expecting —not that I'd ever made out with Juliet before—we'd actually barely had coffee together. We made that one movie, of course, which was how we ended up here.

I wouldn't say I'd made out with lots of women either, but I'd been with enough to know what I liked. And I generally liked kissing. A lot. But Juliet and I were new at this, and there was a fair bit of external pressure—considering the mob surrounding us and the hard-eyed security guard at my back, the one who never let Juliet out of his sight.

It was important to make this kiss searingly hot. Blazing. But it wasn't working, and I worried it might be obvious.

My body—all the parts of my body—stayed nonchalantly relaxed, evidently unaware that I had one of the hottest women in America in my embrace. I gave a soft nip to Juliet's bottom lip and felt her soften in my arms, and . . . there it was. That did it. Not a rocketing surge of excitement, but at least I had confirmation that I wasn't actually dead.

And I guess that was something I already knew about myself. For me, it was usually less about what I wanted and more about making someone else happy. Not just in sex—in life. But when a woman showed me I was making her happy? That was the Holy Grail for me.

Still, Juliet might have made me believe I was having an effect on her, but she was also one hell of an actress. And it didn't matter what I believed. What mattered was what this rabid crowd of paparazzi thought.

"One more for the cameras!" Someone called as we broke apart.

Juliet stood on her tiptoes to nuzzle against my ear as the crowd hooted.

"You're doing great," she murmured. "There hasn't been a single question about my divorce. Grab my boob."

"Grab your ...?" Shock pumped through me.

She tilted her head back and pressed harder into me, and instinct led me to plant a lingering kiss on the column of her throat as my hand found her breast through the thin sweater she wore. She lifted her head to meet my mouth again as my thumb brushed across the upright pebble of her nipple, flashes lighting the stale airport air around us.

If this didn't convince the cameras, reporters, and random tourists we were a hot new item for them to examine, inspect and tear apart, then nothing would. This was some of the singular best acting of my career.

A little part of me wished I did have a thing for Juliet, though if I were actually hoping for an actual relationship, I might be more upset by the ironclad terms of the contract I'd signed with her, stating that this entanglement would extend only through the duration of this weekend getaway with the potential for a short extension on the other side as deemed necessary by Juliet's "people."

Finally, she stepped back and smiled at me, and I got an

up-close demonstration of why Juliet Manchester was considered America's hottest young actress.

She was good.

Her face was flushed, and those green eyes sparkled as she shot me a look that could have been read by others to mean we'd shared secrets and whispers, late night trysts and early morning snuggles.

If I'd seen only the look, I'd almost have believed she was interested in me, except I was the one she'd been kissing, and I knew better.

"We've got a plane to catch," she called to the crowd, pulling me along next to the two burly security guards whose job it was to see us to the plane and beyond.

We pressed through the crowd and checked in. Once we were at the gate, I looked at her as she looped her arm through mine. "I thought the whole point of taking the late flight was to avoid the cameras. You tipped them off, didn't you?"

"My agent did," she confirmed. "You're doing great." She leaned her head into my shoulder and then looked up at me again. "That grope will be all over the Internet by the time we land. We just need to keep it convincing through the next couple days, and we're both golden."

Golden. Right. So why did this all feel so wrong?

CHAPTER TWO
TESS

"How was the movie, my love?" Granny swiveled her head to greet me as I came in and dropped my keys into the bowl on the table next to the door. I crossed the room, planted a kiss on her cheek and slid into the chair across from hers with a sigh.

"Juliet's famous for a reason." I shrugged. I'd never get used to watching my big sister on the theater screen, but there was no question her star had risen and was continuing its meteoric upswing. "The movie was cute, and sappy, and a little bit predictable. But it was good."

Gran made a face, her nose wrinkling and her brows lowering behind her round glasses. "Sounds about right."

I wasn't about to tell Gran about the other video I'd seen Juliet in tonight, the one where Ryan McDonnell was groping her breast in the airport. Gran was no prude—the opposite really. Letting Gran in on that little nugget would only lead to her demanding I pull up the clip and play it for her. And then we'd be analyzing it, Gran critiquing Ryan's kissing prowess and speculating about his abilities in other areas. I wasn't up for it tonight.

Personally, I thought it was a little much, especially considering my sister's divorce wasn't yet final. And because Ryan McDonnell was my all-time movie-star crush, and I was pretty sure I'd confessed that to Juliet before.

She could have anyone she wanted ... the whiny jealous little sister part of me wondered why it had to be him.

Gran clucked at my assessment of my sister's acting. "I told her I'd go see one of her films when she gets to carry a gun and kick some ass."

I grinned at her and sighed. "She does mostly romcoms, Gran." She had done one pretty serious film—it had gotten an Oscar nomination, even. But most of Juliet's movies were light.

"Maybe it'd improve the plots if she had a gun in one of 'em." This comment was followed by a cackle and a snort. "Or some kinky sex!"

I thought again about the airport grope video. If Gran wanted to see Juliet having sex, that was probably about as close as she'd get. Also, ew.

"I'll tell her you said so." I laughed. Gran never bothered to disguise her thoughts, no matter the topic. And she liked movies with explosions and sex. It was part of her charm.

"You better not tell her." Gran's faux-angry expression changed to a quizzical look, her soft wrinkled face softening beneath the trucker cap she wore pulled over her curly white hair. It said "I'm Fancy" on it. I had no idea where she'd gotten it.

"I still don't understand why you like going on your own to the show, Tess. Why not find a friend to go? What about Tony? He's always had a thing for you, hasn't he?" Her eyes searched mine.

"Which is a really good reason not to go to a movie with him." Tony was a friend. Nothing more.

I thought she'd given up suggesting that movies were made for dates. In the small town where we lived, there weren't many prospects for me, and I wasn't really looking, anyway. "I like going alone. I don't feel any pressure to react a certain way and I don't have to share snacks." I leaned my elbow on the arm of the chair, dropping my chin into my hand. "I actually really like being alone. I guess that makes me weird."

"Makes you lonely."

I sat up straight. "Why? Are you lonely?"

She shook her head. "I've got you, don't I? And don't forget Chessy." At the sound of her name, Gran's house chicken let out a squawk from the little dog bed at Gran's feet.

I rolled my eyes at the chicken and then smiled at Gran. "And I've got you."

"Tess, I hate to point out the obvious, but there's an expiration date on that deal." Gran was turning ninety, but I didn't like her to remind me of her mortality. When she was gone, I definitely would feel alone. Since I'd moved back in to look out for her, she was kind of my world. Gran and my job. And I was fine with that, though I guess that made me pretty unusual in the under-thirty set. Most of the friends I'd had in school had moved north to DC or Baltimore, and most of those who'd stayed here had two or three kids by now.

"Don't talk like that, Gran. You're only ninety."

"Not yet, I'm not!" She reminded me. "Not until Saturday."

"True. Well, I guess you can give Juliet your thoughts about her recent roles in person. She's on her way, according to the Internet." Most people learned of family travel plans via email or text. My sister mentioned offhandedly that she would "try to make a flight" a week or so ago, sent a one-line email saying she was working on it yesterday, and then starred in a tabloid video at LAX, confirming she was flying tonight.

"I miss that girl," Gran said, in one of her fleeting sentimental moments.

"It will be nice to have her here for the party," I agreed.

But my mind was turning around other questions. Like, if that video was her on her way here, did that mean Ryan McDonnell was coming too? Or did they bump into each other at the airport? Juliet was barely rid of her losery husband. It was hard to believe she'd have moved on already.

"Did anyone else call to RSVP?" I asked Gran. "And did the caterer call?"

"Maybe." She lifted a shoulder and I stifled my irritation. Gran had a bad habit of pretending to be deaf when the phone rang. It wasn't that she couldn't hear it ring, or that she didn't know how to answer it. She just preferred not to, especially if she was gaming. She also made a stink about the fact we still had a house phone, telling me repeatedly how archaic it made us seem. She did everything on her smartphone and prided herself on how technologically ahead she was of the rest of the old folks she knew.

Gran was her own woman, that was sure. She wasn't like any other almost-ninety granny I knew, though I didn't know many.

I frowned at her, her veiny thin hand resting on the enormous ball of her gaming mouse. Everything in front of her glowed in neon green or blue, except the screen, where her warrior elf was standing, shifting her cartoon weight and waiting for Gran to come back to the game. "How long have you been online today, Gran?"

My grandmother turned back toward me with a guilty expression before swinging her head back to the enormous screen before her. "Not very long."

I waited. She always confessed if I stayed quiet.

"What time did you go to work this morning?" She asked, already sounding guilty.

"Nine o'clock." I'd gone off to teach my morning stand up paddleboard yoga class on the bay, and had been out most of the day since then.

"So ..." Gran drew out the word as if she was doing math in her head, figuring out how long she'd been playing World of Warcraft. "So, only since then."

"Gran!" I stood up, trying to remember that as ridiculous as she could be, Gran was a grownup and I didn't need to lecture her about being irresponsible or lazy. "Did you remember to eat?" It was almost bedtime already.

Another shrug.

"Oh my God, log off right now."

"I've got a guild raid in ten minutes. I'll log off after."

"Gran, the last raid took three hours."

"Now you understand why I'm online for so long." She said this as if I'd just answered my own question and should now be fine with the fact that she'd been playing Warcraft for twelve hours today.

"You remember what the doctor said last week. If it's getting in the way of you eating, you have to stop."

She didn't reply.

"Gran."

Still no answer.

I didn't like to threaten her, but there had to be a limit to how much online gaming was healthy for an almost-ninety year old woman. Right? "I'll get the Internet shut off."

"Tess." She turned in her chair and gave me a frank look, her blue eyes watery and pale but clear and lucid as ever. "It's my house."

"That's low."

"If you make some dinner, I promise to log off and eat with you. Especially if you bring me a Manhattan first."

I sighed. So what if my grandmother had a teensy gaming addiction? And an affinity for rye whiskey? She was old. She'd earned it.

And it didn't seem so bad, really. If I wasn't going to be the marrying type, wasn't going to raise a family, maybe I should look more closely at getting into gaming. I tried not to hear the little voice in my head that reminded me that Gran had gotten married and had her family long before she became a whiskey-drinking online-gaming old woman.

I went to the kitchen to find something quick for a late dinner and to make Gran's drink, staring out the window over the water of the Potomac sparkling in the moonlight as I ran water into the pot for pasta.

I was definitely not expecting the doorbell to ring at this hour, and it pulled me from my late-night dinner prep ruminations.

"Gran did you order something?" I called back to the office as I dried my hands and went to the front door. Gran didn't answer but a raucous bout of flapping and nasal-pitched bawking came from the parlor as Chessy went scrambling for the door.

"Chessy, back," I told her, earning me a beady-eyed glare from the fat hen, who nevertheless took a claw-footed step away from the door.

I peered out the side pane of the door onto the porch, surprised to see two extremely large men in black shirts standing outside.

"Gran," I called, taking a few steps back to where she was undoubtedly immersed in her raid by now. "Gran, did you order football players?"

"Can't hear you," she called, indicating clearly that she could hear me fine. "Gun's in the hall table drawer," she added.

I hated it when she got that thing out, but part of me thought it wasn't the worst idea. We were two women living alone on an isolated piece of land in an old and probably not completely secure house. I pulled the handgun from the drawer with a shiver and went back to the door. It was almost ten PM. Not the time of day when I enjoyed meeting huge visitors.

"Can I help you?" I called through the door, still not opening it.

"Juliet Manchester's security team. Here to check the property in preparation for her arrival." The voice that came back was deep and resonant. And a little bit scary. And super serious.

Chessy made a strange noise in response, cocking her head to one side and letting out a "hmmmm?" Chessy stepped nearer to the door and peered out the side window, looking up at the hulking man who was speaking. She made an appreciative noise in her throat, the one usually reserved for sunflower seeds and anything dropped from the lunch table.

"Oh," I said, unlocking the door and pulling it open. "Sure. Um, come in? Is she arriving tonight? She wasn't totally clear about it." I stepped back, and the two men stood for a moment in the open doorway, their eyes taking in everything.

The chicken.

The darkened house.

Gran's screeched curses coming from the back room as her raid got underway.

And me, holding a handgun.

Chessy interrupted the silence with a loud squawk and tiptoed close to the black boots of one of the men, clucking and circling his feet in a strange kind of examination.

The bigger of the two men frowned at me, his dark skin creasing as his eyes landed on the weapon in my hand.

"Oh, sorry," I said. "It's just…you know, it's late, and… so is Juliet coming tonight?" I shoved the gun into the back of my pants like I'd seen guys do on television. It was extremely uncomfortable and made the waist of my jeans very tight.

"An hour behind us," the other guard said. "Is this a chicken?" He peered down at Chessy, who glared up at him, indignant to be questioned.

"Yeah," I affirmed. "So, how can I help you?"

The first guard, Chessy's guy, finally seemed to relax a bit. He held out a hand. "I'm Jack. This is Christian."

"I'm Tess," I told them.

"Thanks Tess. We'll just check the house and the property line, if that's okay. Just getting a sense for points of potential entry to the property. What's security like here?"

"Um..." I tried not to reveal that me, my gun, and my attack chicken were the extent of it. We didn't worry too much about security.

"Exterior security of any kind? Property fence?"

"No."

"So you have a gun. And a chicken." The tiniest of smiles crossed the man's face.

"And some goats and horses. A couple wild turkeys run through now and then..." I trailed off, realizing too late that Jack wasn't really looking for a rundown of our livestock situation.

"Just secure the weapon please," Jack said. "And Ms. Manchester said bunking here on the property wouldn't be an issue?"

I tried not to let my surprise show. Juliet had invited two security guards to stay at the house, and hadn't bothered to mention it to me? "Sure, that's no issue. So... the two of you."

"There'll be four of us. And then Ms. Manchester and Mr. McDonnell."

A little spike of excitement made my stomach jump. Ryan McDonnell *was* coming here.

With Juliet.

The excitement turned to a clump of hard annoyance. I knew my sister was coming home. I didn't know she was bringing five additional houseguests with her. But I was a Southern girl, and I let that information sink in and absorbed it with a smile. "Well, of course that's just fine," I told them.

"The more, the merrier. I'll just open up the east wing and get some rooms ready for y'all."

I waved the men into the house to do whatever it was they needed to do as I rushed to finish making something for Gran to eat and then headed for the part of the house we generally kept closed off. It would be dusty and dank, but the sheets would be clean.

Once Gran was eating and drinking her Manhattan in the kitchen, the two men finished up their rounds and appeared in the doorway. Chessy was hot on the tail of the one she'd chosen for herself, Jack.

"All set Miss," Jack said. "Ms. Manchester should be here soon."

I watched the two men head for the front door and then I began to sit across from Gran to eat, but the gun down my pants made it all but impossible. I'd almost forgotten about it as I'd rushed around the house. I pulled it out and set it on the table, where Gran eyed it curiously but went on eating.

"What the fuck was that all about?" she asked, a mouthful of pasta barely masking her profanity.

"Juliet is coming. Tonight."

"Ah." The great thing about Gran was that she could accept just about anything without letting it faze her. "Planning to shoot her?"

I rolled my eyes at my grandmother and sipped at my own whiskey. Juliet had a way of stirring things up. Part of me welcomed the change in pace, and part of me resented her assumptions that we'd just mold to her needs, change our schedules and do whatever it was that America's favorite star required.

I washed our plates at the sink and looked out over the back yard.

The water looked smooth and calm as it flowed down toward the Chesapeake past the long gentle slope of Gran's backyard in the shimmering light of the moon. It was peaceful and serene, and as I went through our nightly routine, I pushed myself to feel the same. My life might not be exciting—especially if you were to compare it to my sister's—but it was mine, and it was good. I was happy.

At least that's what I kept telling myself.

CHAPTER THREE
RYAN

Juliet was on the phone almost the entire car ride to a place I could only assume was located somewhere between outer Mongolia and the moon, based on the length of time we'd been driving since landing in DC. This wasn't a part of the country I was familiar with, and once we'd gotten south of the beltway, I was legitimately lost.

I'd checked messages, snoozed and even played a few rounds of Candy Crush as Juliet fielded calls from all directions —her agent, the producer of her next film, and her ex-husband, giving me a pretty in-your-face reminder of how impressive her career was compared to mine.

"I guess I should call my sister," she said after a while, dialing another number on her phone. "Tess," she said into the phone.

I glanced at my watch, a little worried that it was already almost one AM. Was her sister generally up at this hour?

"Yes, I know," she was saying. "I'm sorry about the short notice. And the hour. And about the security guys." She apologized for about four more things and then rolled her eyes to me and made a mouth sign with her hand, opening and closing it over and over before returning her attention to the phone. "Tess, I hear you. And I would have totally given you more notice about Ryan and the guards. It's just ... things have happened really quickly." Now she shot me a look that was clearly an apology to me. Her full pink lips pressed into a line as her blue-gray eyes widened and she gave a tiny shake of her head.

I was beginning to wonder if this whole thing had been a mistake. "Go for it!" My agent had said. "It sure can't hurt your career!" He'd told me. But agreeing to pose as Juliet Manchester's boyfriend was something that might have begged a bit more thought.

Except my career was sinking, and being linked to Juliet—even for a minute—could yank me out of the murk of obscurity and back into view of the directors and producers who seemed to have written me off after my last three action films flopped. And that was without even mentioning the fiasco that was *Charade of Stones*. I'd been on that show for five seasons, my star power growing the whole time, until the writers lost their minds and ended the series by killing off half the main characters and casting the others into obscurity, pissing off every loyal viewer they'd gained in previous seasons. For some reason, the actors were all paying the price for that ridiculousness.

Now, riding in the back of a town car with Hollywood's darling and preparing to pretend we were intimately involved at some family shindig had me thinking I'd just accepted a fairly challenging role.

There was a reporter from *Hollywood Entertainer* magazine coming down to attend the event and document Juliet's 'real life roots' or something, and a new love interest was the one piece her team believed was missing. I'd been in the right place at the right time—or maybe the totally wrong place at the wrong time—and they'd asked me to play the part. So here I was, with the moonlit shadows of hulking trees and barns flying by on either side of me and ... "Was that a horse and buggy?" I asked, sitting up straighter. It was dark out, but the moon was full, and as we sped by the horse and carriage, I thought maybe my tired mind had imagined it.

"Oh yeah, this is Amish country," Juliet said, sliding her phone to her shoulder for a moment to answer me.

"Amish country," I repeated, feeling farther from home than I had since I'd been on location in the Solomon Islands for my last epic failure.

"Hey Ryan," she said, finally putting down her phone and leaning back to look at me. "Thanks for this. I mean it." She smiled, but her eyes stayed sad, distant. "The divorce was such a complete disaster ... I mean, I guess no divorce is a good thing, but everyone just seems to know everything about mine ..." her voice faltered, and I felt the same sympathy I'd felt the night when she'd asked me to meet her at her house to propose the idea. Juliet was a good person. I could help her out.

"It's okay," I said, dropping a hand to take hers on the seat between us. She actually flinched at my touch, which didn't do a hell of a lot for my ego.

After a second she relaxed, leaving her hand where it was. "Sorry," she said. "Just a little tense."

We'd put on a pretty good show in the airport at LAX, and again at Dulles, but Juliet was stiff and rigid. I wasn't sure how convincing our act was going to be, but it was my job to make it work. And I liked Juliet. She was a superstar, but beneath the trappings of fame and glamor, I thought she was a good person. And she'd been treated like shit.

If Juliet—and about a million tabloid reports—was to be believed, her marriage had ended in a pretty spectacular disaster. The husband-banging-the-personal-chef-on-the-kitchen-counter kind. Toss in a little bit of stealing millions from your famous wife, and you've got a picture of what supposedly happened there.

I wanted to do what I could to help show her fans that she'd come through it all without a scratch, even if that clearly wasn't true. Her ex was a leech and a cretin, and he'd siphoned off half her money before she'd walked in on him on the kitchen island. He'd gone straight to the media to play the victim, and they'd caught a few candids of Juliet clearly distraught, leading to a frenzy of tabloid coverage alleging everything from a nervous breakdown to a long-hidden drug habit.

Her shiny new "relationship" with me was a big first step to showing the world she was fine, even though I doubted it was true. When she gazed absently out the window, Juliet's shoulders slumped and the lines around her eyes showed evidence of long sleepless nights.

I found myself wanting to help, even though I didn't have a personal stake in Juliet's life. I didn't like to see people hurting, and if I could help in some way? I would.

"We're almost there," she said, nodding at the passing fields and barns, as if she'd spotted some landmark that to me looked just like everything else we'd seen.

"You ready?" I asked her, our eyes meeting and some kind of understanding passing between us.

My heart went out to her—she looked so sad. Part of me wished I felt something else, that I was interested in her, that my body responded to her obvious sex appeal the way the rest of the red-blooded male population of the United States—and the rest of the world, for that matter—seemed to. But Juliet Manchester, though gorgeous, didn't do it for me.

There was something too shiny, too perfect about her. And I wasn't looking anyway. I'd dated Hollywood starlets, and even regular women I'd met along the journey to becoming Ryan McDonnell. But nothing had ever felt real. I'd always had the sense that each relationship was built for the purpose of one or both people getting something out of it. Every relationship I'd had felt just like this one—forced, a business transaction. This was just the first time the cards were on the table at the outset.

No, if I were looking, it wouldn't be in Hollywood. Some day I'd have enough financial security to leave all that and figure out who the hell I actually was. I'd find someone real and live in a place where people didn't base their estimation of your worth on what your last film grossed or what your address was. For now, that's the life I'd chosen—and it paid well enough most of the time to help me set up a better future. But this weekend, I had a role to play.

"The security team arrived a little while ago," Juliet said. "My sister didn't sound very happy about them scouting the property and poking around the house."

I shrugged. "Necessary evil, I guess." Juliet was a star of the caliber that attracted stalkers and other crazies, so I understood a little bit why we had two burly men in a car behind us and two ahead of us already poking around the house where we'd be staying.

With Juliet's sister and grandmother, apparently. I wasn't sure why we couldn't just stay in a nice hotel nearby, but I was beginning to think it had to do with the totally isolated nature of this place.

Juliet nodded absently. "Once we get settled, it should be just family and stuff until the magazine crew comes out tomorrow. They'll pop in for the party too."

"And are we a couple where your family is concerned?" It would be easier if we didn't have to pretend when the cameras weren't around.

She wrinkled her nose and seemed to think about this. "The fewer people who know we're pretending, the better, I guess."

Great. The pressure just doubled—there'd be no chance to take a breath, let down my guard.

"Is that okay?" she asked, sounding sincerely sorry.

"It's fine, Juliet. That's what I agreed to, right? I save your image, you save my career."

She smiled and laughed, but it was a practiced response. "We'll see what we can manage on both counts."

"So this is your sister's house?" The car had turned between the tall brick posts of a wrought iron fence and was headed down a long gravel drive between two fields of what looked like corn. "Is your sister a farmer?" I angled my head at the crop, shadowed and eerie in the moonlight.

Juliet laughed. "No," she said. "She runs a river adventure shop, actually, teaching people to kayak, stand-up paddleboard, do yoga on the river, that kind of thing. There's a family that lives across the road here that farms the property. And the house is really my Grandmother's, but my sister lives here and looks after her."

"That's nice of her."

"It is," she agreed, though something in her voice was hesitant. "Granny's kind of a handful."

The woman was about to turn ninety. I doubted she could be too much of a handful.

"So it's like a farm? Animals and stuff?"

Juliet laughed, something wistful in the sound as she leaned back into the seat and stared out the window. "Used to have. She loved horses, but can't care for them now. She still has chickens, some goats…"

"Pigs?" I asked. I couldn't imagine a farm without pigs. I'd seen the *Wizard of Oz*, after all.

Juliet's face lost its smile. "No, and definitely don't bring up pigs around Gran."

"Seriously?" I asked. Juliet sounded strangely alarmed and I needed to understand why.

"She hates pigs. Like really hates them."

"Who hates pigs? They're so cute. Look." I pulled up a gif of a pig waving a pinwheel out a car window. "Cute."

"Not cute. She thinks pigs are possessed by the devil."

Gran did sound like a handful, I decided. "Huh."

"Something about being attacked at the Achilles tendon by one at some point."

I had no idea what to say to that, so another "huh" escaped me and I turned my attention back to the windows.

After a moment, a huge two-story brick house came into view, lit up against the darkness, with wings reaching out on each side of the main structure. There were huge trees towering over the smaller wings, casting parts of the enormous structure into shadow. A fountain stood in the center of the circular drive, surrounded by a lawn that rolled around the property and spread out beyond. The whole place was lit up like a national monument. I guess maybe because they were expecting us.

On one side of the house, the lawn reached down a hill and I thought there might be water back there, shaded by trees hanging at the bank.

"It's incredible," I said, my voice holding a reverence I hadn't intended. I'd seen plenty of waterfront property, but this wasn't Malibu. There was something much more stately and reserved about this kind of luxury, about the way it was tucked quietly back here along the shore of a river. I'd never had known Maryland had houses like this or that Juliet had grown up in one. Not that I knew much about Juliet.

"It was a plantation originally," she explained as the car pulled to a stop in front of the house. "The original house was actually built in early 1700, and it's evolved over the years. The British took over the property during the War of 1812 when they blockaded the Chesapeake," she was saying, but my attention was no longer on Juliet's words or on the hulking historic house before us. It was laser-focused on something else. Someone else.

A woman had just stepped out the front door and stood on

the front steps, watching our car with wide eyes, dark hair cascading in waves around her face as the lights caught her in their glow.

Juliet stopped speaking, following my gaze out the window. "And that," she said. "Is my little sister. Tess."

Tess. Everything I didn't feel when I looked at Juliet jumped to attention when I spotted her sister.

The weekend had just become a whole lot more interesting.

CHAPTER FOUR
TESS

Gran had gone to bed by the time two dark cars pulled into the driveway. Juliet had called an hour ago, so I'd been watching for them, unsure how to feel about seeing her with my ridiculous celebrity crush. I bit a nail as I stepped out onto the porch to greet them.

My sister slid from the back seat of the car looking every bit the movie star she was. I hoped everything was going to meet her standards. The security guys had looked around the property for God-only-knew what, and asked me questions about our alarm system (nonexistent), our security perimeter (also nonexistent) and our emergency evacuation CONOPS (seriously? Once they explained what a "CONOPS" was—a concept of operations, in case you're wondering—I explained that was also nonexistent).

My big sister Juliet lived in a world I could barely begin to understand, where movie stars were people you actually knew. People like Ryan McDonnell.

Sigh. Deep, lovelorn sigh.

My sister had never really belonged here, and she didn't fit in any better now, with her huge dark glasses and slim-fitted pink capris and high-heeled sandals. The second I saw her, I felt myself inching toward invisibility again. I loved her, but my life worked better when Juliet wasn't standing at my side, begging the world to wonder how two sisters could be so different.

I pushed down my own insecurities and smiled at her.

"You look great," I told her. It was true. She always looked great.

"Hey," she said in that breathy voice she'd become famous for. She pulled me into a tight hug, smiled at me, and then took a step back, ducking her chin a tiny bit as she said, "I want to introduce you to someone."

A pair of long jean-clad legs slid out of the car behind her, attached to a broad tall body that I already knew too well was Ryan McDonnell. I was more than familiar with this particular 'someone.' He'd been my on-screen crush forever, though I hadn't seen him in anything lately. There had been a movie I hadn't seen—one that hadn't done too well, but it included zombies, which were not my thing, even if you added in Ryan McDonnell hotness.

The object of my movie star affections had bright blue eyes, perfectly tousled dark hair—cropped close now, I noticed—and a body that appeared to have been carved from stone, or so I'd thought in the last role I'd seen him in as a comic book hero reimagined as a dark avenger. God, he was hot.

"Tess?" My sister's voice cut through my stupor.

"Sorry," I said, shaking off the dreamy haze. "Yes."

"Yes?" He asked me, a smile spreading slowly across the perfect lips I couldn't stop staring at. He chuckled, and I realized he hadn't asked me a question. Embarrassment surged inside me, making my stomach churn.

"No," I said, covering my affirmative declaration with an equally unnecessary negative word. "Or, I … um, hello."

"I apologize for the short notice," Ryan said letting my

idiocy slide. People probably acted like loons around him all the time. I tried not to look at him, but there were parts of my body that were not listening at all to my brain. Ryan's smile was like a speeding train coming right at me and freezing me to the spot where I stood, stupid and dazed. "I hope it's not an inconvenience having us both here," he said.

I watched his perfect full lips as he spoke, almost unable to process the actual words. I was having trouble being human, thanks to his actual existence right in front of me.

"Sure," I said, my voice higher than I remembered it being.

More answering questions no one asked. My sister was smiling at me, shaking her head. Juliet knew about my long-time Ryan McDonnell affliction, and it was pretty obvious at this point. I hated that she undoubtedly knew I was flustered just trying to form actual words around her new boyfriend.

I forced myself back to sanity.

"Can I help get your things?" I had no idea if it would be weird to acknowledge his status as my favorite actor or if it was rude to pretend I had no idea who he was.

I settled for a moronic silence on the topic.

Juliet put her arm around me. "You don't need to get the bags," she said lightly, as two of the men from her security team emerged from a second car, all black T-shirts and muscled arms pulling suitcases from the trunk.

Of course not. My sister had people for that.

I'd given the security guys a few rooms in the east wing of the house. With only Gran and me here, we barely even went into most of the rooms on that side, but I'd managed to get a few rooms decent. The house was hardly celebrity material the way we usually lived, the two of us moving mostly through three or four rooms. Gran had talked me into setting up her gaming computer in what had once been the formal parlor because it was the warmest room in the house and Gran was always chilly. The setup—with her dual monitors and the noisy fan-cooled computer coupled with her gigantic ergonomic gaming chair—hadn't really contributed much to the general décor or historic feel of the place, though, and I'd spent the last hour moving it since talking to my sister about some magazine feature Juliet thought would be happening this weekend.

I couldn't wait for Gran to wake up to find I'd moved her beloved computer.

"I wasn't sure where to put you," I said, looking at my sister as we entered the house and headed upstairs to the west wing after pointing out the east side to the security crew. "They're over there, and I set up the two rooms across the hall from each other up here for you." Those rooms had been ours when we'd come to visit as kids. "I wasn't sure if you and, er … Ryan, would be sharing a room."

There was a question in my voice, and I wished I could reel back time and sound a bit more confident, but there was an unfamiliar feeling ricocheting around inside me.

I was having a hard time believing that my sister was dating Ryan McConnell. And that she hadn't mentioned who exactly she'd be bringing, just that she had a new boyfriend who'd be joining her. If I hadn't seen the Internet video, I'd have been far less prepared than I was now for meeting Ryan. At least, with a bit of notice, I'd been almost verbal. If I'd had no idea and he'd just popped out of the car like that, I probably would've fainted.

"We'll take them both and play it by ear," she said, smiling at Ryan with her eyes aglow, shimmering like they shared ten thousand secrets together.

My stomach churned with what I was horrified to admit was jealousy.

Ryan reached out and traced a gentle finger down her cheek, returning the look.

"Um. So." I wasn't sure if I was intruding by speaking

when he was looking at her like that. I cleared my throat. "Are you hungry? I mean…it's late, but you've been traveling."

"I'm okay," Juliet said. "Tired mostly. Ryan?"

He shrugged and smiled at me, "I can always eat. But if it's any trouble, I can wait until breakfast."

"No trouble," I said, something multi-legged spinning around inside me, making it hard to stand still as it jigged and jumped.

"Do you mind helping him find something?" Juliet asked. "I might just go to bed early."

"Yes, well, sure…" I was still not coherent. This wasn't good.

"Okay, great," Juliet said, giving Ryan a quick kiss on the cheek and heading into one of the rooms I'd set up for them.

"I might just grab a quick rinse to wash off the flight," Ryan said. "I'll be five minutes," he said, grinning and then disappearing into the bedroom behind me. The one Juliet hadn't gone into, which seemed a little odd, but I was too busy trying to recover my ability to speak to worry much about it.

I tried hard not to think about the fact that he was very likely taking his clothes off in there, stepping into the tiny bathroom for a shower. Ryan McDonnell. Naked. In my house.

Juliet stepped back out of her room, frowning. "I just realized I didn't really even get to say hi," she said, pulling me into a hug. "I hope this is all okay, having Ryan and me."

My sister held me tightly and I closed my eyes, inhaling the scent that I remembered, her nearness erasing all the distance created by the fact that she lived all the way across the country and was more famous than the president. She was still my big sister, and I'd missed her. For a long time, we'd been partners and best friends. And it was good to have her back.

"It's fine," I said. "It's good. Gran will be thrilled to see you."

"I wish it wasn't so late. I want to say hi, introduce Ryan."

"Tomorrow," I said. "Although she's going to be pretty pissed off because I moved the game rig to the back of the house."

Juliet's mouth formed a little "o." "She's still obsessed with that game?"

I lifted a shoulder. "Pretty much."

"I thought you were going to wean her off of it." Her eyes narrowed at me.

"She's so mean when I don't let her play." I heard the whining tone in my voice and tried to squash it. "I figure there's not much harm. She's ninety years old—who am I to tell her what she can and can't do?"

"It can't be good for her," Juliet said.

"She doesn't smoke as much pot when she's playing," I pointed out. "So I think it's actually good for her health."

Juliet shook her head, one blond tendril escaping her messy bun and falling down around her cheek.

"So this thing with Ryan," I said, walking around one side of her bed to smooth a fold in the duvet I hadn't noticed before. "Is it pretty … uh … serious?" I hated the way my stomach clenched as I waited for her answer.

She pressed her lips together and glanced to one side before she answered, and then gave a quick shake of her head. "I don't know." She threw out a false little laugh.

Something was up. That was the Juliet trifecta. She might be the country's most popular actress, but I could see through her. The side-glance and the lip press were hallmarks of a Juliet Manchester untruth.

"What aren't you telling me?" I took a step closer.

"There's nothing to tell, Tess. Zac was a shit, and now I'm seeing Ryan." She turned. "I'm exhausted. I'm going to bed. We'll talk tomorrow."

"Good night," I said, my mind still trying to work out what she wasn't saying. She didn't seem as excited as I would be to be dating the hottest man on Earth. I left Juliet in her room, and stepped into my own room a few feet down the corridor.

I needed a moment before I could attempt to act like a normal person and help Ryan find something to eat. I stepped into my own room's ensuite bathroom and closed the door behind me.

I stared into the mirror. I could handle this. I could figure out how to form coherent words around my sister's new boyfriend, and I could figure out how to stifle the pointless jealousy I felt that of all the men in the world, she had chosen him.

It was ridiculous to be jealous. That's just how her life was.

But it was difficult for me ever to prepare myself for the churn of feelings my sister stirred up in me. It was like the second she was near, I shrank down and became invisible. Now, as grownups, I felt like I should have been able to hold my own. I wasn't an insecure teenager anymore, after all. And I loved my sister, I really did. But she had a way of sucking all the air out of a space, of pulling every eye and mind and leaving no room for anyone else.

And God, having her here with Ryan McConnell? I was going to be a disaster all weekend.

"It'll be fine," I told myself. "Once you get past your fanatic crush and see that he's just a normal person, it'll be fine."

He was just a normal, very hot person who, of course, probably loved my sister.

And why wouldn't he love Juliet? Everyone always had. Hell, even I loved Juliet in a ridiculously overprotective and self-sacrificing way. That was just the effect she had on people. That was what compelled people to her on screen.

It was kind of like the effect Ryan had on me. I would have been happy just to watch him move. Hell, I'd be happy watching him breathe.

"Tess?" I heard his deep voice just outside my door and my heart hammered into action. So much for normal.

"Yes, coming," I called back, my own voice sounding high and bizarre, like a crazed squirrel. I stepped back out into the hallway to find him standing in a fitted white South Bay Sharks T-shirt, a pair of dark jeans, and his hair wet and pushed away from his face. He smelled like soap and something else I could only describe as absolute manly perfection. With a hint of mint.

"I'll show you the kitchen," I managed to say. I found it was easier to speak to him if I didn't look at him. Or breathe. Or think too much. "We've got some leftovers from dinner."

I turned and we went down the stairs, my hyperawareness of Ryan's presence at my back making me feel dizzy and loopy. Still, we arrived in the long galley kitchen without incident, and I waved toward the little table at the side of the space.

"This house is amazing," he said, wandering the length of the counter and peering out the windows toward the back yard. At the end of the counter were bags of flour and cans of cherries and a huge block of dark chocolate I'd gotten from the little chocolate store in Leonardtown. "And whatever is about to happen here looks pretty amazing, too."

"Oh, that's going to be a cake," I told him. "If I can figure out how to actually bake."

He looked over his shoulder at me, shooting me a smile that might have actually caused my panties to disintegrate.

I was so screwed.

"I'm a decent baker, actually," he said.

"Really?"

"Black forest cake?" He asked, holding up a can of cherries.

"Gran's favorite." I was leaning against the counter next to the refrigerator, my arms crossed over my chest as I considered him. I didn't really need new reasons to appreciate the man, but if he could actually help me make the cake I'd promised Gran, I might be willing to add baking to the things I loved about him. "I ordered a bunch of decorations to put on top… but the actual making of the cake might be a little beyond me. I can cook. But baking…"

"Consider it done," he said, putting down the can and smiling. "Maybe I can earn my keep here for the weekend."

I was about to respond when I heard some kind of commotion coming from the east wing of the house, just to the other side of the kitchen. Chessy was upset about something. "Ah, just a minute," I told Ryan, turning to find out what had the hen indignant at this late hour.

I found her clucking outside one of the bedrooms I'd set up for the security team, pacing back and forth. She stopped when she saw me, squinting up at me.

"You're coming on too strong," I told her. "You can't throw yourself at him. And you can't force your way into his room, Chess." I scooped her up, and she settled against my chest, seeming to accept my chicken-crush wisdom. "Let him get some sleep," I suggested. "You can charm him tomorrow."

I carried Chessy back to the little dog bed where she slept, which I'd tucked beneath an end table in the parlor when I'd moved Gran's computer. We'd have to move this before the magazine people showed up too, I realized.

Back in the kitchen, Ryan was poking around, investigating things. He looked so handsome with his slicked back hair, his strong broad chest. I could have just watched him forever. But he caught me staring.

"That sounded… odd," he said, the bright smile lighting his eyes.

"That was Chessy. Gran's pet chicken."

Ryan nodded. "Pet chicken. Right."

"What? You don't have a pet chicken that lives inside your house and develops misplaced crushes on the security teams that pop in ahead of your famous sister?" I grinned.

"No, I do not," he said. "I'll look into that. Hadn't considered chickens as possible pets."

I looked around to make sure Chessy hadn't followed me in. "I don't recommend them. Very needy."

He chuckled, and then looked back toward the cake supplies. "So do I get to bake?"

"You don't have to, but it would actually be amazing to have help. You wouldn't think it would be a big deal, but the cake has to be really big, and I'm not very confident. I watched a YouTube video, though, so it's probably a sure thing."

"Well, then I'm sure you'd nail it." He moved closer to me, that smile still working it's magic on every female part of my body from my earlobes to my pinkie toes. I felt like I was humming. Inside. With my vagina.

"Great. Okay. Um... I made pasta for Gran tonight, is that okay?" I worried for a minute he might be on one of those Hollywood diets Juliet had told me about before. Keto or vegan or non-GMO or non-soy, or all kale all the time, or... something different than the stuff I made for Gran.

"I love pasta," he said, and the words sounded genuine.

"Go ahead and sit," I said, again finding it was easier to talk to him if I ignored the devastating smile. And the face that went with it. "I'll just heat it up real quick. Do you want a beer or something?"

"Any chance of a glass of milk?"

I poured a glass of milk, barely able to handle how much that simple request had skyrocketed my attraction for no real explicable reason. Was it because it was just so American? So boyish? So...real?

I set his food in front of him with a slice of garlic bread, and slid into a chair across from him, worried the proximity might somehow send me into a hysterical fit. Or give me a case of the vapors or something, if those were an actual thing. Maryland was technically the South, after all.

"This is amazing," he said through a mouthful. "And wait," he took a bite of bread. "Did you bake this?" He narrowed his eyes as if he'd caught me in a lie about baking.

Oh how I wished I had in that moment. "Nope. I get it at the little local farmer's market."

He nodded knowingly, and for a minute neither of us said anything. There was a warm glow from the lights above and a faint buzzing pulse from the cicadas outside, and something about sitting in a quiet kitchen as Ryan ate felt homey and safe. I felt my nerves begin to calm.

"Never been to Maryland before?" I asked him.

He looked around, as if the kitchen might be representative of the whole state. "Nope. First time. You grew up here, right?"

I nodded. "You'd never know Juliet Manchester was from a place as far flung as this, right?"

He tilted his head and looked up at me, the dark lashes around the blue eyes striking. "Not surprising really," he said. "There's a lot of beauty here." This was delivered looking straight into my eyes, and a shiver went through me at his words.

He was talking about Maryland. Which was definitely beautiful. Or maybe he was talking about Juliet. Who was also beautiful.

"Yeah, there's so much water, and it's just really green and lush…"

"That too. Tell me about the house," he said, taking another bite.

I leaned back in my chair, thinking about how much I loved this old house, the stories it held. I decided to tell him one of my favorite things about the place. "Have you ever heard of a priest hole?" I asked.

The fork paused halfway to his mouth, and he shook his head lightly. "Sounds kinda dirty, Tess."

I laughed at that, enjoying the intimacy of the joke and the way he said my name. "It's not, I promise."

"Darn. Okay, well tell me then." Half his mouth lifted in a wry smile and then he took another bite. "Did I mention how good this is?"

The way he was looking at me was not helping my focus. My skin was heating and I had the urge to flex muscles I didn't think of often. Deep, inside, neglected lady muscles.

Juliet's boyfriend, I reminded myself.

"Okay, well, I get carried away with this stuff, so stop me if you know this. Maryland was settled in the 1600s by a guy they called Lord Baltimore, and he was a Catholic."

"Okay," Ryan said, encouraging me.

"His real name was Cecelius Calvert, and he was fleeing persecution of the Catholics in England."

"Or he might have been fleeing persecution of people who named other people lame things like Cecelius," Ryan pointed out.

"Very judgy," I chastised.

He laughed. "Go on. Sorry. I'll hold my judgment over dudes from the 1600s with chick names."

"Okay. Good." I was warming to the telling of my tale, encouraged by Ryan's warm laugh and intent gaze. "So he settled Maryland, but it didn't stay mostly Catholic for very long. When they figured out they could grow tobacco here, a lot of low-cost labor was brought in, along with businessmen to run operations, and soon the Catholics were a minority.

"So anyway, there were years of struggle between Catholics and Puritans, and eventually there was a Maryland Revolution that went on for two years. At the end of it, the colony was placed under royal control, and the Church of England was made the official church, so Catholics were being violently pursued, killed and run out."

"Oh oh."

"Yeah. So many of the original families down here were Catholic—descendants of the original settlers that came over with Calvert. And they were sympathetic to the priests who were being targeted directly, so they hid them in these secret hidey-holes called 'priest holes.'"

Ryan looked mildly disappointed, his lips and eyebrows pulling slightly down. "Not dirty."

I laughed. "No, but I think it's cool. You want to see it?"

"I've never had a gorgeous woman offer to show me her priest hole before."

I crossed my arms again and shot him a look. I'd offer to show him lots of things if he weren't Juliet's boyfriend. The words 'gorgeous woman' ricocheted around in my brain, but I kept them in a little cage up there to think about later.

He raised his hands. "Okay, sorry. Yes, definitely. Let's have a look."

I led Ryan to the pantry. "In here."

I opened the door and pulled the string to turn on the single bulb inside, and then bent down to roll back the rug covering the floor. There was a trap door below it, the outline barely noticeable in the hardwood planks. I pushed my fingers into the corner where there was a slightly bigger space, and pulled the door up.

Ryan knelt down on the other side of the door, and we both peered into the dark space, which was really not much more than a hole cut into the earth below.

"That's really cool, Tess," he said, looking up at me across the space. His intent and open gaze made my stomach flip.

"Isn't it? They used it for the Underground Railroad too."

"No shit?"

A laugh rolled out of me, low and happy. No one ever wanted to talk history with me, and it was fun to see Ryan seem to truly appreciate my little diversion. "Yeah, no shit."

"I love history," he said. "We have history out west, you

know. But it's not the same—not ours really. Not American, exactly, you know?"

"I'd love to go out west," I told him, closing the door again. He reached out and helped me smooth the rug over the floor, and then we stood.

Suddenly, I was inches away from Ryan McDonnell in a space no bigger than most closets, his chest just a few inches from my face. My heart skittered as I looked up at him to find him smiling down at me, something flickering in his eyes. In any other situation, I would have said it felt like heat, like interest, like some kind of nearly sexual intensity between us. But this was not just some guy. And this guy was not available.

And I was definitely imagining the energy drawing me closer to him.

I stepped back, bumping into the shelves behind me and sending a couple cans crashing to the floor. The noise broke the strange moment into fragments that skittered away like mice, disappearing into the pantry's dark corners as we righted the cans and went back out into the kitchen.

"Did you get enough to eat?" I asked Ryan, unable to look at him now, for fear I'd fling myself into his arms.

He cleared his throat, swallowed loudly. "Yeah, uh. Thanks, Tess. That was great."

I took the dishes from the table and walked to the sink. I needed to get back up to my room, to get some distance. The late hour and the headiness of being alone with Ryan McDonnell was doing things to my mind.

"I can wash those," he said, stepping up next to me.

"Don't be silly," I told him. "You're company. And we have a dishwasher."

He stood there a long minute more as I rinsed the bowl and glass, and then he stepped away. "Okay, well. I guess I'll head up to bed then. Should we bake tomorrow?"

I turned to face him.

Mistake. Whatever I'd felt in the pantry was still there, burning in those eyes when I met them with my own.

God, how did women function around this man?

"You don't really have to help with that," I said quickly. I was certain he'd just been being nice. "I mean, I've got YouTube and the recipe."

"I'll help. Tomorrow, okay?"

"Yeah, okay. Thanks." How would I survive baking a cake with him? I wanted to throw myself into his arms, could I manage mixing and sifting instead?

"Great." He shot me another smile, and turned to go. At the doorway, he said, "Tess?" God, my name on his lips was like the nicest song I'd ever heard. It was better than *Pitch Perfect* and I was obsessed with that movie.

I turned to find him lingering just inside the kitchen. "Yeah?"

"It's really nice to meet you."

And then he was gone.

I collapsed into the chair he'd sat in and dropped my head into my hands, unable to process the amount of time and words I'd just shared with Ryan McDonnell, the movie star. This was not my life.

I just wished I could keep my mind from embellishing everything that had just happened.

He had definitely not been giving me a look in the pantry, right? He was Juliet's boyfriend. And in my experience, when you had champagne, you didn't go looking for moonshine.

CHAPTER FIVE
RYAN

I woke to sun streaming through the tall windows of my room, and I stretched in bed and lounged longer than I probably should have, enjoying the lazy lack of anything I absolutely had to do.

Sleep had come pretty easily, despite the unfamiliar location and bed. I was tired, for one thing, and that helped. The stranger thing, though, was that I felt oddly settled here. At home. And that was something I hadn't felt in a long time. Maybe ever.

I suspected some part of that had to do with Tess, but I couldn't have explained exactly why.

When she'd gotten me dinner, there had been something so natural about spending time with her, talking with her in the cozy old kitchen with its warm light and hidden spaces. This house—more than that, even—this place… it spoke to something inside me in a way I couldn't understand in any terms that made sense. But I knew I liked it here. A part of me already felt sad that soon I'd be going back to the plastic people and shiny spaces that made up my regular life.

Sure, there were great people and real things in Hollywood. But so much of my world was made up of people focused on things that just seemed somehow impermanent and flimsy to me. My own quest for stardom … what would it get me? Financial security, I hoped. And security for my dad. But beyond that? Look at what Juliet was going through, all in an effort to keep her reputation clean in the eyes of the world, all to stay on top in the minds of people who didn't even know her.

In another life, I'd have considered making a place like Maryland home. Maybe I had lived here in some previous life, hiding priests in tiny holes and growing tobacco like Tess said. But I'd chosen my home and my life for now. And the financial promise of the path I was currently walking made it pointless to think about things like this. Hell, maybe I'd known Tess in some past life, too. How else could I explain the way I felt around her, the closeness I sensed was already between us?

Or maybe I was just longing for the kind of life I couldn't have. At least not now. It didn't stop me from thinking about it though, about what it would be like to live here with a girl like Tess in this quiet beautiful place, maybe open a little restaurant someday.

After lounging in bed a while, I thought I could hear Juliet talking with her sister in low voices somewhere outside my door. I glanced out to see them both heading for the stairs and couldn't resist the urge to let my eyes trail down Tess's back as she disappeared from sight. Juliet was beautiful, but her sister was in a completely different class.

The hot-as-balls class, if you wanted to know the truth. The class that made my blood pound a He-man rhythm through my veins and my nether regions come up with ideas that were altogether inappropriate, given that I was supposed to be dating her sister.

Where Juliet was an indisputable beauty, her appeal was very obvious, almost in your face. Her sister, on the other hand … something about her made you want to look longer.

From the long angles of her nose and chin to the round pout of that small mouth. She wasn't tall, and she wasn't short—she was perfect, as far as I could tell. She moved away from me, having no idea I was tracking her every move. Her body was curvy and generous, and everything about the way her hips moved as she walked made me want to drop my hands to her waist and feel the motion for myself—maybe pull it into me.

If I was honest, Tess's body made me think of dirty, dirty things… but I forced my mind away from them and chastised the parts of me that insisted on obsessing about what it might be like to feel her close and tight and hot around me as my hands filled themselves with her perfect breasts.

Even though she was physically perfect, that wasn't the thing that made Tess so strangely compelling, and I realized it wasn't any one thing—it was everything I'd learned and seen so far. I realized I barely knew her, but something fundamental inside me had responded the second I first saw her, and now I seemed to be nursing a serious fixation. It was a little unsettling, actually, because I was a guy who spent long days around Hollywood starlets, and I'd never been more taken with anyone than I was with this girl I'd found practically in the middle of nowhere.

I wanted to know her. To have the privilege of learning her.

There was the small issue of having to pretend to be smitten with her sister, however. But, I told myself there was no reason I couldn't learn a little more about Tess Manchester on a purely platonic level while fulfilling my duties to her sister. And this little ruse wouldn't last forever.

It wasn't long before Juliet came up to get me for lunch—

I'd been catching up on email and general news in the room. Something about being so far from a big city made me feel oddly out of touch, despite the fact that we'd left Los Angeles just the night before. It wasn't an altogether unpleasant feeling, actually.

"Come meet Gran," she said, leaning against the doorframe.

"Anything I need to know?" I tensed a bit at the thought of telling our lie to an elderly family matriarch. I wanted to make a good impression.

While lying, of course.

Juliet tilted her head to one side and then wrinkled her nose before speaking. "She's quirky."

"Quirky how?"

"You'll see."

Juliet wasn't lying. Gran, who I'd expected to be a frail old woman with maybe a cane or a shawl over her shoulders, was decked out in a designer sweat suit, looking a lot more Beyoncé than Grandma Moses. She was bent over the counter by the sink, giving a silver cocktail shaker a workout, when Juliet called out to get her attention.

"Gran, this is Ryan," she said.

Gran looked over her shoulder with an appraising look and then turned back to her task, pouring a brown concoction into a martini glass before putting down the shaker and wiping her hands on her pants as she faced us. "Hello," she said, smiling sweetly. "I'm Helen, but everyone just calls me Gran, so you might as well join in."

"It's a pleasure," I told her, shaking her small thin hand gently. "Thank you so much for having me."

She gave me a narrow-eyed look then, and I got the distinct impression I was being evaluated. "Do you smoke pot?" She asked.

Juliet stifled a laugh and I shot her a look, trying to figure out if there was an appropriate response I didn't know about.

"Um, no ma'am. I mean. Once? In college? I didn't inhale, of course." I felt my face reddening.

"Right," Juliet laughed.

"You do coke?" Gran was escalating her investigation, and I wondered exactly where we were heading. What was the right answer here? I got the sense it might not be the one I would normally default to around parental types.

I swallowed my surprise and shook my head. "No ma'am. I've got a pretty serious Altoids habit I've been trying to kick, but I'm clean when it comes to opioids, narcotics, hallucinogens and whippets."

"Whippets?" Juliet asked, her eyes wide.

"Yeah," Gran said. "Whipped cream cans? You've never done one?"

Juliet's brows lowered at Gran's explanation. "Seriously?"

"I think we're having pie later," Gran said. "I'll show you."

"Um…" Juliet said.

"So no, ma'am," I said, trying to distract from Juliet's worry over the potential that later we'd all huff whipped cream cans in the kitchen of this old plantation house with her elderly grandmother.

"Pity," Gran said, turning back around and picking up her drink. "Manhattan?"

I glanced at the clock behind her, noting it was barely noon. "No thanks," I said, almost wishing I did feel like a drink. The lady of the house was no doubt full of surprises and I looked forward to sitting down to learn about her life here in this place.

"Lunch on the porch," she proclaimed, and we followed her out a screen door to a wide sweeping back porch overlooking the lawn and the smooth water flowing beyond it.

"This is incredible," I said. I'd had no idea Maryland

would be so beautiful. "Is that… the Chesapeake?" I took a guess.

"That's a river," Gran said, and she sat down clucking her tongue. "Californians." She shook her head.

I thought about whether I wanted to take a guess at which river it might be, but I also found myself wanting Gran to like me, and my lack of drug use and ignorance of Maryland geography had me feeling like I was behind the power curve.

"Ignore her," Juliet said. "It's the Potomac."

Juliet waved me to a seat, and we each served ourselves from the center of the table. I glanced around, wondering where Tess was, but I didn't want to ask. Giving Juliet the impression I was interested in her sister was probably not a good idea. And I wasn't exactly interested in her. I mean, she was interesting, no doubt.

I suspected it was more that I was fundamentally drawn to her. I'd actually never felt anything like it, and I didn't trust the feeling completely. Maybe I was just tired? Maybe I'd feel completely ambivalent around her when we next saw one another.

Maybe, I thought, I felt around her kind of the way I felt about waffles when people first set them in front of me—super excited, like I'd never had anything half so good. But within three bites, I regretted the waffle decision and kind of wished I could just have something else.

Maybe Tess Manchester was just a regret waffle. So to speak.

I sighed and turned my focus to my lunch.

"So you can't screw things up too badly, I'd guess, on the heels of that last asshole, Juliet," Gran said. She was clearly talking to Juliet, but she was looking at me.

"Gran!" Juliet's tone was scolding, but there was laughter in her smile.

"I'm pretty sure I told you back then that Zac was a

moron, but no one ever listens to me," the old woman continued. She sipped her drink and then looked at me. "Just wait, young man. Once you hit a certain age, everyone assumes you've got a few connections unhinged up here—" she pointed at her head, "and they pretty much ignore everything you say."

"We don't ignore you, Gran," Juliet said, her eyes wandering to follow a couple of security guards out toward the yard. A chicken was following so closely behind one of them it was a wonder he didn't step on it.

"Chessy!" Gran yelled, looking out at the chicken. "Leave that poor man alone!" She snorted and took a swig of her drink before turning back to Juliet, pointing a potato chip in her direction. "Well if you listened to me, you wouldn't have married that idiot in the first place. And please tell me the media was wrong about the settlement you're giving him. My whole guild is talking about it. That numb-nuts didn't deserve a cent." She sipped her drink again and then leaned toward me conspiratorially. "That moron was a couple beers short of a six pack. Hope you're firing on all cylinders, cuz he certainly wasn't." She turned her fierce gaze back to her granddaughter. "So, the settlement?"

"Did you say guild?" Juliet asked.

"Yes. In the game." Gran waved a hand, clearly not ready to be distracted from her question. "Settlement. Talk, young lady."

First Juliet looked a little shocked, as if she'd been slapped. "I don't think you can 'young lady' me anymore, Gran." Then she sniffed and dropped her gaze to her plate. "I'd rather not talk about it," she said. "It's not final, and it's just … it's hard." She looked up again, a brilliant smile plastered over the pain in her eyes.

My heart went out to her, and I remembered again how well Juliet covered her real emotions. It was rare to see her shield slip to reveal her sadness over her current situation. I reached over and took her hand—more because she looked like she needed it than because we were supposed to be a couple.

And Tess appeared in the doorway at that exact moment, and I couldn't have explained why, but I snatched my hand back as if I'd been caught doing something I shouldn't. Juliet shot a surprised look my way and I smiled, realizing Tess Manchester was definitely not a regret waffle. It would be easier if I could just turn the feelings off. But I suspected it wasn't going to be that easy.

Tess stood in the doorway for a moment, her dark hair around her shoulders as her gaze went out to the lawn where the chicken was now flapping and clucking around at the feet of the guard, who was actually trying to run away from it. Tess wore a pair of jeans rolled around mid-calf—the kind that were beat up in a sort of intentionally casual way, and a tank top that showed off her curves but definitely looked like a shirt she would have simply pulled from a drawer, not something she planned. She was beautiful in such a natural and effortless way, it actually made me gasp under my breath, trying to get myself under control.

I glanced at Juliet, but she didn't seem to notice my struggle.

Tess carried her plate to the table and sat next to Gran. "Poor Jack," she said, looking out at the chicken and man on the lawn. "Chessy won't leave him alone now. It was love at first sight."

"Jack?" Gran asked. "Is that one of the gorillas that came with these two?" She tilted her head to mean Juliet and me.

"Gran, behave yourself," Tess said, her tone admonishing but full of sweetness. Her eyes sparkled. "Juliet and Ryan are celebrities. They need security, and while they're here, we're lucky the guys were able to be here too."

"Hmph," Gran grunted. "And by the way, I'm not speaking

to you today, about goons or anything else. I can't believe you moved my stuff." Gran's voice had all the indignity of a maligned teenager and when she stuck out her tongue at Tess to make her point, I had to stifle a laugh.

"I said I was sorry about that. But it's for the magazine shoot tomorrow. It's just temporary. And so are the guards." Tess sounded exasperated.

For the most part, our security detail was practically invisible—a significant feat for four guys who must've weighed two hundred and fifty pounds a piece.

"So," Tess said, turning to face Juliet and me. "How did you guys meet?"

"At a party," I volunteered, at the same moment that Juliet blurted, "On set."

I cringed inwardly. This was what we probably should have figured out before arriving. Tess didn't seem easy to fool, and Gran definitely didn't. I wondered if Juliet might decide we could just be honest with her family and keep the pretense for the media.

Tess raised her eyebrows and laughed, and the sound filtered through me like sunlight sifts down through tree leaves, soft and diffuse.

Juliet raised her eyebrows at me, as if to tell me to continue, so I improvised. "It was a party on the set of a movie we both worked on," I said. "We had one scene together, but didn't really get to chat until the wrap party." I knew it was a poor cover and watched Tess consider this and decide not to question it.

A faint smile ghosted her heart-shaped lips. I had a fleeting vision of what it would be like to rub a thumb over those lips, to taste them. I refocused on the sandwich before me. *Wrong sister. Focus.*

"When was that?" Tess asked.

This time, Juliet and I looked at one another, and I decided to let her answer. We should have ironed out all the details ahead of time, but she'd slept through the flight and she'd been on the phone through the car ride. These were things we needed to get airtight before the magazine people showed up. If we got this wrong in front of the media, Juliet's scandal would be even more scandalous and I'd be an easy target for stories about poor desperate Ryan McDonnell who'd do anything to save his career. That would not be good for me, or for Dad.

"The movie went on about six months, so we've known each other a while. But the party was just a little while ago. Two weeks?" Juliet said, looking to me to confirm.

"Sounds about right."

Gran snorted and leaned back in her chair. "So this is your third date?"

"Gran," Juliet sighed.

"Two weeks?" Gran repeated. "I've got hemorrhoids with more mileage on them than that."

Tess dropped her sandwich back to her plate. "And I'm out." She stood and shot Gran an angry look. "You're impossible."

Gran merely shrugged and continued nibbling her own sandwich. I watched Tess go, wishing I could follow her into the house, but I was supposed to be here with Juliet.

"It is new," Juliet said. "But it feels … right." Her delivery was good. I didn't get a chance to see if Gran was buying it because my eyes were on Tess's back as she went back inside the house.

Or if I was being honest, my eyes were on her ass.

I waited as long as I could, something inside me ramping up and forcing me out of my seat. "I'm just gonna go visit the bathroom," I said, rising and dropping a kiss on Juliet's cheek.

"Be right back." I slipped through the swinging screen door behind Tess, my mind spinning and my heart in my throat. I had no real idea why I was chasing her or what exactly I was going to say. I just knew I wanted to talk to her. Alone.

CHAPTER SIX
TESS

I had just turned on the water to rinse my plate at the sink when Ryan came in the door after me, a strange expression on his gorgeous face. I was still a little annoyed—Gran was legitimately impossible, and I was worried what she might say in front of the magazine people when they arrived.

I turned to face Ryan, a nervous hitch in my breath.

"Sorry about Gran," I told him. "She can be a little …" I trailed off. There was really no word for Gran. "She's not great in company, but on a daily basis, she's a pretty entertaining companion."

"I'd guess so," he said, leaning against the counter next to the sink, his eyes on me and his gaze intense. There was something in the way he was looking at me that made me feel warm all over, little shudders of excitement popping through me.

I slid the dish into the rack and looked up at him, feeling nervous as the bright blue eyes pierced me. I felt weirdly naked, exposed. "Is there something I can help you with?" It was difficult being this close to him. The attraction I'd always felt seeing him on screen was magnified about six thousand times having him just eighteen inches away from me.

"Well," he said, his voice low and soft enough to make me tilt in toward him so I didn't miss a word. He leaned a hip into the counter, his body close to me, his eyes never leaving my face. "I thought we better talk about cake."

The kitchen was quiet, but the air was filled with some kind of energy, a buzz that filtered between the atoms around us, made me feel like I was levitating just the tiniest bit. I stood there at the sink, staring into Ryan's eyes, and had the strangest sensation—like he was about to kiss me, like something had to happen between us just to relieve this strange tension. Just when I feared I might do something insane like throw myself into his arms or reach a hand out to trace that perfectly clefted chin, Juliet came through the door.

I stepped back instinctively, like a kid being caught doing something naughty.

"Gran's crazy," she said to me, not seeming to notice the thick heady air in the kitchen, or the way my chest seemed to be struggling with each breath.

I felt dizzy and slightly sick when I looked away from Ryan. "Yeah." I made a point of avoiding his gaze, moving away from the magnetic pull of his body. "So I'm going to get the tractor and start pulling the chairs and tables from the barn in back. And then I'm making a cake." I glanced at Ryan, who smiled at this, like we shared a secret.

"The caterers aren't doing that stuff?" Juliet looked vaguely annoyed at the thought of manual labor and baking.

I shook my head, wiping my hands on my jeans. "Nope, just the tent. Now that it's up, I've gotta get the stuff in there. They're going to arrange it tomorrow morning."

"I don't know why you didn't just let them do everything." Juliet rinsed her dish and slid it into the rack. Ryan was still watching me. I could feel those piercing eyes on me, and a sheen of sweat was threatening on my brow. It was going to be a very long weekend, since I couldn't seem to manage to behave like a normal person around him.

"Money, Juliet. It's a way to save money." I shrugged and glanced at Ryan, who I was sure didn't have to worry about regular-people things like money. But I wasn't about to pay someone else to do something I could easily do myself. I pulled my shoulders up straight, pushing away the heat of embarrassment that was replacing the warmth that had flooded my cheeks just moments before.

Juliet waved a hand, as if she'd heard enough, saying, "I'd help, but I have a few calls I have to return and then I need to start reading lines for my next movie."

Liar. She'd never been big on helping if it meant the potential to break a nail or a sweat. "It's fine," I said, refusing to be annoyed. My sister was here for one weekend. I could deal. "Is Gran done?"

Juliet shrugged.

"Can you sit with her until she goes back for her rest, please?"

"Sure," Juliet said, but she sounded distracted, or put out, like she had something else she needed to be doing. But she didn't leave, she just stood, staring out the window at the lawn where the guards still patrolled.

Ryan had been quiet this whole time, standing nearby, watching me. Suddenly he said, "I'll come help you with the furniture and then we'll make cake."

My eyes slid to him, even though I knew looking his way was dangerous. Why would a movie star want to do manual labor? Juliet definitely didn't.

That got Juliet's attention. "You don't have to do that stuff, Ryan. My sister just insists on being a martyr sometimes," she said.

I frowned at her, trying to figure out what was making her

grumpy. She had always been work-averse, but she'd never really been mean. "What?" I asked.

Juliet's expression changed immediately, and she reached for my hand, looking sad. "I'm sorry, Tess. I'm just...I'm really wound up and distracted. All this divorce stuff..." she trailed off, shaking her head.

"I'll help," Ryan said again. "I'm happy to." He was too handsome, and my body seemed to have a mind of its own when he was close. I should have been listening to my normal, sane mind. The one saying: movies stars who are dating your sister are not fair game no matter how they are looking at you.

And he was looking at me in a way I could only call ... hungry.

Man, he was a good actor. I knew he was acting—or just kind of naturally wore an "I want you" kind of look, because historically, any man who'd shown interest in Juliet did not find himself looking at me in a hungry kind of way. We were like chocolate and vanilla—people only had only one favorite. And it wasn't usually whichever one I was. Was he playing some kind of game? Trying to impress my sister by being nice to me?

"Tess." Juliet bumped my shoulder, forcing me to realize I'd been staring silently at Ryan McDonnell instead of answering his offer of help like a sane person might do.

I cleared my throat. "Okay, yeah," I said, even though I knew it would be best to stay as far away from him as I could. He was just being friendly, and my body was reacting as if he'd invited me to bed, my lady parts all hot and wet and my mind running all kinds of scenarios that featured him and me, and had little to do with setting up chairs and tables or baking cakes.

I wanted nothing more than to spend time with him, but I wasn't sure I could trust myself. "I'll be out back in the barn. Right there. The" —I pointed to the left side of the back yard, where the hulking red form of a barn was evident through the window— "the barn? Over there?" Oh my God, I was losing my mind.

"Hard to miss the enormous red barn out back," Juliet muttered, turning to leave the room.

"I'll be right behind you," Ryan said, grinning at me. "Gotta do one thing first."

My knees actually weakened with the force of his smile, and I spun on my heel and went back outside before I did anything insane. I'd never experienced this level of intense reaction to anyone before—was it chemical, maybe? I'd heard about that, but my body didn't seem to have gotten the memo that no matter how the chemicals he put out influenced mine, he wasn't mine to react to.

I crossed the yard and calmed myself during the course of the long walk. I was being ridiculous. Ryan was just being helpful and friendly, and my years-long movie-star crush was clouding my brain and making me believe there was something more to it. It had been months since I'd dated, and longer since I'd actually done anything more than kiss someone—if that ridiculous desperate kiss I'd let Tony get one night at the local bar counted.

As far as I was concerned, it didn't.

And kissing Tony, a guy I'd known as long as I'd known myself basically, was not anything that should be put in the same realm as kissing Ryan. Not that I'd kissed Ryan.

My sister's new boyfriend.

Oh God.

My body was clearly just going haywire after abstaining from sex for so long. I took some deep cleansing breaths as I pushed open the barn door and pulled the utility cart from where it leaned against the wall. As I attached it to the back of the small John Deere tractor, I was feeling better.

Work. I just needed to do some work.

This was my life. Work and home, me and Gran. There was nothing else—

"What can I do?" Ryan's deep voice rolled through the dusky interior of the old barn, and my stomach tightened again, my blood heating immediately. So much for my newfound calm. He'd changed into loose-fitting shorts and a T-shirt, and had running shoes on and a cap on his head. He looked sporty and athletic, and I had an irrational urge to climb him and wrap myself around those broad strong shoulders.

I cleared my throat and stood, "Hi."

He grinned and my heart shot off in a crazy double-time rhythm as my palms slicked with sweat suddenly.

Fucking chemistry.

"Um. Yeah. So." Since words were not working for me, I pointed across the space to where the tables and chairs were all stacked and hung on pegs against the wall. We'd once rented the property's grounds out for weddings, and we still had all the tables and chairs in here, so I'd planned to use them for Gran's party. But maybe I should have let the catering company get this all set up, as Juliet suggested. It was going to be a big job.

Ryan crossed the space and pulled a half-round table from the front of the stack. His muscles bulged and strained with the effort, and I was having a tough time breathing, even though I was only watching.

"Crap," I muttered under my breath, angry at my traitorous brain, which wouldn't stop suggesting ways I might get just a bit closer, maybe run my hand along one of those muscly muscles.

Juliet's, I reminded myself. He is Juliet's.

"Here," Ryan dropped the table into the cart attached to the tractor and grinned at me. I could watch this all day, I thought, my breath shallow and all the blood rushing through me heading directly for the places I wished I could rub up against this man.

"Good, thanks." I swallowed hard and forced my feet to move toward him while I kept my inappropriate impulses under control. I'd agreed Ryan could help me; he hadn't volunteered to move all the furniture himself while I stood nearby drooling and panting. I went to help, and together we hoisted six tables into the cart, filling it completely.

"You drive this thing?" Ryan asked, running a hand over the tractor's steering wheel.

"Yeah," I said. "It's the easiest way to move things around the property."

"I've always wanted to drive a tractor," he said, looking impressed.

"You can drive if you want. It's not hard." I showed him how to get the engine going with his foot on the brake, and which pedal would move him forward.

He gunned it toward the door of the barn and hooted. "You coming?" He called over the noise of the engine. Ryan McDonnell was full of surprises. I'd never seen anyone excited over driving a tractor, but the guy looked like he was getting to take the best rollercoaster at the amusement park.

"I'll walk and meet you over there." I shot him a questioning look. There was only room for one on the seat.

"Get in back!"

It wasn't a good idea—the tables could shift around and there was barely anything to hold on to, but his smile had me making questionable decisions. I climbed on top of the tables in the cart and grabbed the sides as Ryan gunned the tractor again, pulling us out of the barn and across the wide expanse of lawn to the huge white tent the catering company had erected the day before. A silly smile covered my face as we bumped across the yard, and giggles flew from me as Ryan swerved around, clearly enjoying the drive. I felt like a little kid again, holding on for dear life.

He was hollering and laughing, and I was reminded of the way I'd felt suddenly when he'd asked for milk the night before. Like he was a guy who didn't feel he had to be a grownup all the time. Like he knew how to have fun. When he switched off the engine in front of the tent, I was still laughing, and it helped ease some of the strange tension I'd been feeling around this man.

This movie star.

This hot new boyfriend of my sister's.

We unloaded the tables and popped them up, not worrying too much about where they got placed. The caterers would arrange things. I headed back to the door of the tent when we were done. Ryan had gone out a second before, and I shot a final glance over my shoulder at the space to make sure it was all still intact after sitting out here all night. I should have been looking where I was going, because I bumped into a solid form in the doorway. Ryan had been standing there, watching me.

"Woah," he laughed, his hands catching me by the arms, steadying me.

Walking while looking in the other direction was not one of my advanced-level skills, evidently.

I spun, and suddenly I was two inches away from him, his hands on my arms and our faces close enough that I could feel his breath on my forehead. All the rushing blood and butterflies I'd managed to banish while we'd been setting up tables came slamming back into me, making me feel giddy and warm.

"Sorry. Thanks," I breathed. My mind spun deliriously, but at the same time, a calm overtook me—a focused calm that had me staring at Ryan's lips, feeling them pull me near despite my best intentions.

He stared at me, his blue eyes darkening and something in his face changing from a question to an answer.

His hands slid from my arms to my waist, his big fingers wrapping around me, his thumbs slipping low over my belly. Warmth spread through me at his touch, and those intense blue eyes burned as they stared into mine.

As if in a dream, he angled his head down slowly until our lips were centimeters apart.

I didn't breathe. I didn't move. I didn't think.

Until I did.

I took a step back, forcing my body out of his reach, away from the magnetic pull of his orbit. This was not some fantasy. Ryan was my sister's boyfriend, and my sister had been hurt enough. Plus, I was about as far from my sister as a guy could get. No one was interested in us both. It didn't happen. Which meant I was definitely losing my mind.

I narrowed my eyes at Ryan. He hadn't been about to kiss me, clearly. Had he? What the hell was happening?

I took a deep breath. "I'm uh ..." I could barely form words. I shook my head. "Okay, well. Thanks," I pushed past him out the door and seated myself on the tractor. I needed to escape, get some space to think and regain control of my traitorous body. I'd just started the engine when I felt the whole machine jolt beneath me. Ryan had jumped into the cart and he was grinning again.

With no idea what the hell had just happened, I engaged the gas and drove us back to the barn. We spent the next hour loading chairs and running them across the lawn in the tractor. Neither of us mentioned the strange moment in the doorway or said anything else, and I pointedly kept my eyes and body focused in one direction to keep from crashing into him again.

By the time we finished up and Ryan told me he'd meet me in the kitchen to bake the cake after he took a quick run, I had almost convinced myself I'd imagined the whole thing.

And I hoped I had, because if I hadn't imagined it, that meant I'd almost kissed my sister's boyfriend, and my sister didn't need anyone else in her life being shitty at the moment. It would also mean her boyfriend had almost kissed me.

And that was pretty shitty too.

CHAPTER SEVEN
RYAN

I ran along the road leading back out of the Manchester property, my mind reeling. On one hand—the primal side of me that had just been close to kissing a woman I had a very chemical attraction to—I was stoked.

Being close to Tess was heady and exciting, and imagining her body beneath my hands, her sharp wit and sparkling eyes close to me, it only made me want so much more of her. There was something intense and old and complicated in the air around me and Tess, something demanding to be explored.

But on the other hand, I'd made a commitment to her sister. And while the relationship was fake, my promise was not. I was a man of my word in a world where those seemed pretty rare. I wanted to be a man of honor, even if everyone else in the world thought that was old fashioned.

Even if our game of pretend was stupid, there was something in it for me. And blowing this would mean potentially blowing my chance at reinvigorating my flagging career, and gaining the financial security I needed to take care of my father. And exposing Juliet to the ugly rumors and speculation that had surrounded her since her sudden divorce. That didn't seem very honorable.

My feet beat a steady rhythm down the unfamiliar road as my heart and lungs pounded along. Lush greenery arched overhead, and a surprising variety of critters scattered as I passed—fat little groundhogs nosing at the edges of the road, more birds than I'd ever be interested in identifying, rabbits hopping beneath the towering trees, and a few deer who paused in the road to watch me approach before loping gracefully into the protection of the dense woods beyond. I was completely charmed by Maryland. I'd thought this backwoods location might be boring, but instead it was full of surprises.

Not the least of which was Tess Manchester.

I continued down the road, picking up my pace until my mind could do little but focus on the run. Sweat trickled over my skin and my lungs screamed, and finally I reached more water—by way of a wooded property that led to a sloping sandy beach at the end of the road. I stood for a time on the beach, watching the water lap at the shore as the sun reflected off the liquid surface in flashing diamonds.

By the time I'd returned to the big house, I'd settled with myself. I had to behave myself while we were here, and that meant being true to Juliet and our arrangement. But I also planned to get to know Tess—through conversation only—in an effort to see what this thing was that was undeniably between us. I'd follow the rules, which would mean ignoring the driving demands of instinct every time I was near Tess, but I could do that. I might have decided this once before, but this time I meant it.

I could absolutely do that. Besides, I was not about to break a promise. I knew too well what it felt like to have promises broken, and I wasn't going to do that to anyone else.

I let myself back into the big house, nodding at the security guards stationed by the door.

"Hey," one of them said, stopping me from walking right by.

"Hey," I replied, turning to smile at the guy. He looked a bit like a regular guy until you noticed the muscles bulging beneath the dark T-shirt he wore. "It's Jace, right?"

He nodded, and leaned his head toward the other guy. "That's Chad."

"Thanks for being here, guys. Looking out for us." I wasn't used to round-the-clock security, but it felt weird to just accept their presence and not acknowledge it.

"We're here for Juliet," Jace said, his voice deep and a little bit terrifying.

"Right, yeah," I said, feeling sheepish now. I hadn't been implying that I was so important they were here for me. But I wasn't surprised these goons thought I was just another entitled Hollywood asshole. "Just… thanks."

Jace sighed, and Chad muttered, "any time." Then Jace said, "Juliet was looking for you a while ago."

Worry pricked inside me that I might be messing up on my promise already, and I thanked Jace and hurried through the door.

I went upstairs to shower and to find Juliet. She was in the room across the hall, pacing and talking into her phone. I waved and pantomimed that I was going to shower. And I should say here, that while I am an excellent actor, a shower pantomime is particularly difficult.

She wrinkled her nose at me, her eyebrows dipping over those gray-blue eyes. "What?" she mouthed.

I upped my shower-acting game, picking up an imaginary bottle of shampoo, squeezing a bit into my hand and then washing my hair, whistling all the while.

See? I can act, no matter what the critics say.

Her eyes cleared in understanding and she smiled, mouthing, "got it."

When I was done, I went back to her room to see what she'd needed while I'd been out running, but her door was closed. I considered knocking—we were definitely nowhere near the just-barge-in stage. But I wasn't sure a closed door was really an invitation. I raised my hand to rap my knuckles on the wood, but I thought I heard her moan softly in the room beyond, and my heart went out to her. Was she crying? She'd had a rough time lately. If she was taking a nap, or even having a cry, she definitely deserved it, and I wasn't going to interrupt.

I wandered down to the kitchen, and I felt the smile cover my face and work its way through the rest of me when I spotted Tess at the counter, wrapped in a pink apron and leaning on her forearms on the counter watching a YouTube video about making big cakes.

She had gotten out a few oversized pans, and they were lined up on the counter.

"We better prepare these bad boys," I told her.

I saw her shoulders stiffen as she pressed pause on the video and straighten up. She turned to me with a grin that actually made my knees wobble, then looked back at the lined-up pans, lifting a finger to shake at them. "Okay, pans. Here's what's going to happen. First, we're putting cake batter in you and you'll need to hold it all inside, okay? Then we'll be sticking you in a hot oven and hoping for the best. This is going to be an important cake, so don't mess it up."

I stifled the laugh that wanted to come out, along with the urge to take her in my arms, to push my nose into the hair at the back of her neck. I chuckled, waiting until she looked up at me for approval.

"Not exactly what I meant, but that was a good first step."

She raised her palms as if to say, "I did my best. They're as prepared as they can be."

"I meant by greasing them. Or better yet, lining them with parchment paper."

"I don't think we have any papyrus around here," she said.

I raised an eyebrow at her. "Seriously?"

"Okay, fine. I know what parchment paper is." She went to the pantry and came back with a big roll of it. "I use it for baking fish."

"That sounds interesting," I said, taking it from her. "Maybe you can teach me that sometime."

I refrained from slapping myself. I shouldn't be making future plans or trying to give her the idea I wanted to make plans with her. I could spend some time with her, ask some questions, get to know her. Not make plans.

"Sure," she said, and I heard the hesitation in her voice too.

We prepared the pans, buttering, flouring and lining them, and there was a quiet companionship between us that I found myself trying to soak up and savor.

It was an odd thing, I realized. Being a celebrity meant there were millions of people in the world who "knew" me—but I spent much of my time alone, and even more of it feeling lonely. It was rare to have a quiet moment shared with another person, to be able to enjoy something simple, something pure.

Tess didn't push me to talk, and together we measured, mixed and poured, and before long, we had the first of the pans in the oven.

"Where did you learn to bake?" she asked as we cleaned up.

I sighed. Every story about my past was lined with landmines. How much did I want to share with her? I started off slowly. "I didn't. I just started doing it after my mom left. It reminded me of her, I think. She used to bake. Kind of taught myself."

Tess's face changed, her lips pressing slightly into a frown. "Did you bake with her? Before?" Her tone showed that she wasn't going to press, wasn't going ask why Mom had left.

Relief wound its way through me, but so did a vague disappointment. Why did I want to tell Tess everything?

"We baked a little. Cooked, too." We sat down, neither of us verbalizing our intention to do so. But as with all things with Tess, I was finding we seemed to agree naturally, to be in the same mental space, maybe. "She wasn't a very happy person, I guess. So I don't have a lot of memories of doing things together. A few."

"And cooking is one of them? So maybe that's why you like to do it?"

I took a deep breath, let it out. This wasn't stuff I was used to talking about. The facts, maybe. But not my feelings about those facts. "Maybe. I never really thought about it."

She nodded. I wondered if she was contemplating what we had in common—we'd both lost mothers. Though I thought Juliet had told me they'd lost both their parents.

"What about you?" I asked her, realizing she might stand up and walk away. I was asking a very personal question of a woman I barely knew. "Do you have happy memories? Of your parents?"

Her eyes met mine then, and I felt myself leaning toward her. I wanted something I couldn't define, something she made me feel. A sensation ran through me I could only classify as yearning, and I wondered if I'd ever actually felt it before.

"I do," she said, and a little smile crossed her lips, brightening the golden eyes. "A lot. Me, Juliet, my parents. We were happy," she said. She didn't volunteer more, and I didn't push, and for a while we sat silently. I thought about my mom, and imagined maybe Tess was thinking of her own childhood.

"So when you're working," I began. "You kayak? Juliet said you were an adventure guide."

She nodded, the eyes brightening again. "That's right. Kayaks, canoes, stand up paddleboards. If you can do it on the water, I'm on it."

I narrowed my eyes at her. "Anything? Water skiing? Snorkeling?"

"Yes and yes." She rose to my challenge, her chest pushing forward as she crossed her arms.

"What else?"

A laugh escaped her. "Name it. We just started doing yoga on stand up paddleboards."

"That sounds more like swimming." I imagined myself attempting a yoga pose and toppling off the board into the water.

"That's why we wear life jackets," she said, smiling. "Want to try it?"

I wanted to try pretty much anything that would find me with Tess Manchester wearing a bathing suit. "Sure."

She grinned, but then her face dropped. "We've got these cakes to finish," she said. "And by the time they're done, it'll be getting dark."

My heart jumped a bit at her clear disappointment. Did Tess want to spend time with me the way I found myself looking for reasons to be with her? "I'd love to try it sometime," I said, realizing I was making plans again. My stomach saved me, offering a distraction with an audible growl.

"Maybe we should eat something."

"I'm not super hungry," she said, "but I can find something for you."

"I'm always hungry." I grinned at her. "I can hunt for a snack if that's okay. You don't have to go to any trouble."

"No, you sit. I have some crab cakes in here, I think." Tess was already pulling a plate from the refrigerator.

I sat up straighter. Yum. "Crab cakes?"

Tess brought the plate my way to show me the tasty round mounds and my mouth began watering. "Did you make these?" I asked her.

"I make them every week. Gran likes to have them pretty regularly. Do they look okay to you?"

"They look amazing."

She heated them for a minute or two in the microwave, and I watched her move around the kitchen, trying not to be obvious. She was graceful and strong, and I wanted to know everything about her. After a moment, Tess put the plate down and then sat across from me, watching me as I began to eat.

"This is amazing," I told Tess, pointing my fork at the crab cake on my plate.

"Well, it is what we're known for," she said, her voice almost a mocking song. "You come to Maryland, you get crabs."

I raised an eyebrow, unable to keep the grin from my face. "That should be the state motto."

She laughed, and a blush crawled up her neck, spreading over the line of her delicate jaw. When she laughed, it was a breathy sound that pulled at something inside me and made my stomach jump. "You know that's not what I meant."

I chuckled and kept eating, but sensed she had something else to say. I glanced at her, a silent invitation to talk.

"So this afternoon," she began. "In the tent ..."

She was going to ask me about those few heady seconds when she'd been so close I could just catch that delicate jasmine scent coming from her skin, when I'd let my eyes drop to her plump pink lips, slid my hands around her little waist, and actually thought about kissing her. I'd been a second away from letting instinct take charge—when my better judgment had kicked in. Or maybe Tess had stepped away.

Either way, I was not here to romance hot little sisters. I was here to get the boost being associated with Juliet would give my career. I was here to be her costar in the promised film being cast when we returned. Even if my heart had begun trying to elbow my mind out of the way to take charge.

"Yeah, so, glad I could help with that," I said quickly, hoping she'd go with it.

She shook her head, her adorable brow wrinkling and a breathy laugh coming from her that made me wonder what other breathy sounds I could get her to make. "Okay." She frowned, seemed to decide something. "Yeah. Thanks for helping." She stared at her cup for a long minute.

Then she set her teacup on the table and peered up at me from beneath dark lashes. Her almost ebony hair was pulled back into a loose high ponytail and I couldn't help imagining my hand wrapped in that dark hair, my body pressed up against hers. "Look, Ryan. I'm not a movie star," she continued. "I don't live the lifestyle you and my sister do, and I don't know what's typical in Hollywood, California. I'm more familiar with Hollywood, Maryland, and—"

"There's a place called Hollywood, Maryland?" I didn't really mean to interrupt her. But once I had, I thought I might be able to derail the dangerous train she was heading my way.

"Yes, actually. It's just north of California, Maryland." A little smile lifted one corner of her mouth.

"There's a place called California, Maryland?" This was a strange state.

She nodded. "I know. It's weird."

"Weird," I agreed, glad we seemed to be veering away from discussing what had happened in the tent that afternoon.

Just then, the oven timer dinged, and I stood, maybe too quickly, to pull the first pan from the oven. With cakes this big, I didn't want to put more than one pan in at a time.

"How's it look?" she asked, peering over my shoulder as I set it on the cooling rack. She wasn't touching me, but it didn't matter. Every cell in my body lit up at her proximity and my dick decided this cake-baking thing was some kind of complex foreplay and that maybe now was a good time for him to wake up. I'd had enough trouble calming the guy down after the barn earlier.

I took a wooden skewer and inserted it in the center of the pan, pulling it out clean. A totally misplaced pride washed through me. I didn't fail in front of her. So there was something.

"Looks good," I said.

"Here we go." She slid the second pan in, and I closed the door once it was settled, moving back to my seat.

"Look, the thing is," Tess said, picking up the thread of conversation where the timer had interrupted it. "I just ... I'm not used to being around movie stars, I guess. It's just, I mean the way you touched me this afternoon..." Her eyes met mine and there was something vulnerable in her gaze, so pleading and innocent—I felt something protective shift inside me, a feeling I needed to hold firm. She was not mine to protect.

She shook her head, as if to force her thoughts to fall into line. "Things are just pretty simple here most of the time, that's all."

"You fucking hackers!" Gran's voice came from somewhere deeper in the house, causing my head to snap toward the doorway. What in the world?

"Is she ... um, should we go check on her?" Gran was an interesting character. I didn't know what she was up to, but I was starting to like her almost as much as I liked her granddaughter, Tess. Although right now Gran sounded pretty angry.

"No, she's fine. It's her game."

Game? I wasn't sure what game Tess meant, and just as I was about to ask, Gran's voice came again.

"You can't fucking camp the spawn! You can't camp the spawn, you fucking hackers!"

Tess just smiled at me, her eyes dancing. "You really shouldn't camp the spawn. It's not polite."

The question I was about to ask must have been clear on my face as I started to smile, and Tess answered quickly.

"World of Warcraft. She's addicted."

"Oh," I said, the confusion turning to amusement as I leaned back in my chair. "I had a roommate in college who played that. He ended up failing out. Never went to class."

"He was probably camping the spawn," she suggested, grinning.

"Must have been." I wasn't entirely sure what that meant, though I'd played my roommate's game a few times, but I'd sit here joking about it all night if it meant getting to see Tess smile like that again. The warm feeling I'd had being in this kitchen with her the night before returned. It was homey and close, and so fucking right it terrified me.

I needed to watch myself. It would be so easy to lean into this reassuring comfort. But Tess wasn't the Manchester sister I was supposed to lean into.

"Sorry. She's nuts. But she's happy, so …" Tess smiled. "Look. I don't know exactly what happened outside today. Maybe I hallucinated the whole thing."

I was about to jump in, to let her know that she definitely didn't hallucinate it. The memory playing on constant loop in my brain, and the way my dick jumped to attention every time I let myself focus on that memory could attest to that.

But Tess went on. "I shouldn't even tell you this …" she laughed lightly, one of my favorite sounds. "I'm probably just bound to read too much into things because I've had this ridiculous movie-star crush on you literally forever." That laugh again.

My body stirred to life when she said this, my heart doing a little tap dance in my chest. "Seriously?"

The blush brightened her skin again, and I had to grip the edge of the table to keep my fingers from chasing it up her cheek. "Yeah," she said, shaking her head lightly. "So maybe it makes it hard to separate reality from years of seeing you in movies. But you're with my sister. So maybe don't touch me. It's just confusing, you know?"

I nodded, sure the pain of my disappointment must show on my face. She was right, she was only telling me what I already knew. So why did I feel like I was losing something? "Yeah, of course. I'm sorry, Tess."

I was. I was sorry for putting her in a situation that had made her uncomfortable. I had to do better. Somehow.

"I'll hold my fan-girling back, but in small towns like this, you can't just go around … touching people." She said this as if she knew the idea that I'd almost kissed her had absolutely nothing to do with some misguided belief on my part that it was totally normal behavior. She was giving me an out.

"I'm really sorry, Tess. I shouldn't have touched you like that. It was just… it kind of felt like there was a moment out there, and …" I wanted to tell her how my blood rushed when I stood near her, how my mind stopped turning when that light scent of hers wafted my way. "I guess both Manchester sisters are pretty irresistible."

Her face smoothed, becoming an inscrutable mask as her shoulders stiffened. She blew out a little breath that sounded a lot like frustration, and I had the distinct sense I'd put my foot in my mouth. "I mean, no. That isn't what I meant." But it was too late. Her eyes blazed as she took a breath and fixed me in my seat.

"Can I ask you a question?" She said after a brief silence.

"Yeah, of course." My voice revealed just a hint too much of the longing I felt for her. I wasn't sure if she heard it.

"You came here dating my sister, nearly kissed me earlier, and just told me the Manchester sisters are essentially interchangeable in your mind. Don't you think that makes you a bit of an asshole?"

Oh God. Is that what I said? It wasn't what I'd meant to say at all. "I think it came out wrong."

The light did not come back into her eyes and I had a sudden desperate churning feeling in my stomach, like I needed to fix this immediately.

"I'm not sure there's a right way for that to come out. This is a small town, Ryan. Maybe we do things differently here than in places like Hollywood. We're careful with people's feelings." She paused, straightening her shoulders. "And if you hurt my sister after everything she's been through ... or if I find out you're just using her..." she trailed off and the warning in her words lingered in the air between us.

"I don't want to," I told her, guilt flooding every cell in my body and sending the semi-erection I'd had all through our baking adventure wilting like an ashamed flower. Because wasn't that the deal I'd made? I was going to use Juliet, with her permission, to advance my own career, to land myself the financial security I hadn't found so far. "Of course," I said, my stomach twisting with what felt a lot like a lie.

"Good," Tess said, standing and carrying her cup to the sink. "Well, thanks for your help with the cake, movie star Ryan McConnell. I can get it from here."

I was being dismissed. And even though it made my heart ache to realize it, maybe it was for the best. I made a promise to Juliet. And I needed to keep it. Spending too much time with her sister, no matter what my soul seemed to be telling me, would only complicate things.

"Okay," I said. "Okay, sure."

I turned and left the kitchen, heading back upstairs to try to get my head on straight.

I couldn't let my heart move closer to Tess Manchester and still honor my contract with Juliet.

CHAPTER EIGHT
TESS

I finished baking the cakes myself, feeling the quiet and emptiness around me—it almost felt as if things had gone back to normal. Just me here on my own, Gran screeching intermittently at her computer, and Chessy flapping around here and there. Though Chessy had been distracted since Juliet's entourage had arrived. But even with four guards and two movie stars in the house, it was easy to feel at this moment that I was just as alone as usual.

I let my mind trace over the events of the day so far. I'd be lying if I didn't admit that the moments in the barn and tent were the most exciting I'd had in years. Maybe ever. But Ryan's words, about both Manchester sisters being irresistible, kept coming back to me too. And I kept reminding myself what a shitty thing that was for him to say—or at least how shitty it was to act on it, to assume that just because he was Ryan-fucking-McDonnell, he could almost-kiss whomever he liked.

What bothered me most was that some part of what he'd said didn't feel entirely true. And he didn't really seem like an asshole.

I couldn't explain it, but something in my gut had clenched

at his words, had signaled that something might be off. But I doubted I could trust my gut where hot movie stars were concerned, and besides, it was unlikely that anyone interested in my sister would look twice at me. In fact, I'd had plenty of experience with guys who'd seemed interested in me at first then suddenly became interested in my sister after meeting her.

I'd even had a guy I was dating fall in love with my sister after she'd moved away. He'd fallen for her when she wasn't even here—when there was no real possibility of him even meeting her. He'd found out my sister was the famous Juliet Manchester, and become convinced that if he could just hang around long enough to meet her, she'd fall for him too. Gran had taken care of that guy for me, ushering him directly back out the front door with the gun in her hand after I'd told her what was up.

"You deserve better, Tessy," she'd said, waving the barrel around over our heads as if to make her point.

I'd taken the gun from her and tried to smile, wishing my heart could believe her words as much as she seemed to. I didn't know what I deserved exactly. But maybe years of being jealous of my sister had poisoned karma against me. Maybe I deserved to be alone.

I hoped that wasn't true. And I was tired of being alone. Being with Ryan today had been strange—but nice. I was wildly attracted to him, sure. But even as the initial shock of hanging out with the actual human version of my movie star fantasy had begun to wear off, there was something really nice about being with him, if I just overlooked the way it ended.

Nice wasn't really the word I wanted to use. It was so much more than that. It was heady and powerful, basic and simple. It was like I was supposed to be with him, but I knew that didn't make any sense.

Because Ryan was Juliet's boyfriend.

I could hear them talking in the front room with Gran as I

pulled the final layer of cake from the oven. I'd frost and decorate it tomorrow.

Dinner was going to be simple. I grilled some fish, made a green salad and put a pitcher of lemonade and one of iced tea in the center of the table, and then wandered the house, calling out that it was dinner time. Two of the guards came in the front door, and Chessy's favorite, Jack, was already out on the back porch.

"Shoo, chicken," he said waving his hands down at Chessy. But when I poked my head out there to see if anyone else had come down yet, Chessy was running at him, butting her head into his shins, a sign of chicken affection. I called up the stairs, and heard doors open and feet moving. After stepping through Gran's new gaming room and having a small argument about her being in the midst of a quest, she came outside. It was early enough in the summer that it wasn't stifling hot, and when the breeze picked up off the river, the mosquitos weren't too bad.

The meal was quiet. Juliet mostly stared off into the distance, looking haunted and sad, while Ryan didn't say much either. Gran shoveled her food down and then stood.

"I'm missing a raid tonight," she said, sounding grumpy. "I thought y'all would be more fun than this. It's like everyone's practicing for starring in some shitty soap opera. Is *"Life Sucks and Then You Die"* filming here tomorrow? It's supposed to be my birthday this weekend!"

"Gran!" I said, wishing sometimes I could slip something into her Manhattans to make her more polite.

Juliet stood and went around to wrap Gran in a hug. "I'm sorry Gran. I'm distracted."

"What's his excuse?" She asked, pointing at Ryan. "Or theirs?"

The four big men at the table looked embarrassed and muttered apologies before turning back to their food.

Ryan actually blushed, and shook his head lightly. "I apologize, ma'am. I've been a terrible guest." He looked between Gran and me as he said it, as if part of that apology was meant for me. My earlier anger had already softened, and now I found it hard to locate at all.

"Hmph." Gran wasn't letting this go easily. Evidently she'd expected quite a bit more entertainment from our famous guests than she was getting.

"Maybe I could mix you up a drink, Gran?" I offered, which earned me a dirty look from Juliet. I didn't like Juliet being annoyed with me, but she wasn't here most of the time. I'd learned how to mollify my grandmother to keep things peaceful around the house.

"We should play Monopoly," Juliet suggested.

"You call that a game?" Gran sniffed. "I'll take my drink, Tessy, and I'm going online. Y'all better be a lot more fun for the party. I didn't live this long to have to try to figure out what everyone around me is moping about."

As Gran left the porch, sniffing, Juliet sighed and dropped her head into her hands. A little knot formed in my stomach as I realized now I was somehow responsible not just for keeping Gran happy and sedate, but I also had to worry about my sister disapproving of the way I did it.

I rose and followed Gran into the kitchen. I purposely didn't look back at Ryan, and I didn't return to the table after I'd set Gran up with her drink. Instead, I went upstairs to read, and was in bed nice and early.

I WOKE up the next morning early and dressed quickly. I wanted to get a workout in before any magazine crew craziness got rolling, and I thought a decent sweat session might clear my head, which was still muddled with movie star almost-kissing, intimate baking, chickens with mad bodyguard crushes and

Juliet's weird moping. It was too much to worry about, so for now I was going to focus on getting my heart rate up and banishing some worries with sweat. I'd left the watersports shop to the employees to run for the rest of the weekend, and felt free and light, despite all the chaos and strangeness in the house.

I padded down the stairs to the basement, switching on the lights and ignoring the boxes stacked against the unfinished walls on the side beneath the stairs. That was storage, which was what this space was probably intended for. Most houses around here had basements, but the ones built as early as ours didn't usually have the high-ceilinged, finished affairs that newer houses did. The ceiling down here was high enough to hang a heavy bag and a speed bag, but only because I wasn't a tall girl. They would have been comically low for anyone over five-four.

I moved to the center of the floor, where I'd installed some pads, and jogged in place for a few minutes before beginning to jump. I mimed jumping rope—something the ceiling was too low to actually do—and watched the clock. When I'd been moving for five minutes solid, the sweat beading at my brow and my breath coming fast, I took a few minutes to stretch out, moving the whole time. When I felt loose enough, I got to work, going through the same series of punches and kicks I'd been doing forever, moves I'd learned from my dad, who'd once been a Golden Gloves champion.

He'd taught me to box when I was a tiny kid, as a way to feel powerful in a school system where being a scrawny mousy-haired girl didn't always allow you to feel that way. Juliet had gotten along fine—being beautiful from age one would do that for you. But I'd always been a little different. And while I'd never minded not fitting in with all the other kids, it seemed to bother them a lot that I didn't care. And I'd needed to learn how to make them leave me alone. Maybe words would have

Happily Ever His

worked better, but Dad knew how to use his fists to convince people of things, and that's what he'd taught me, perhaps against my mother's wishes.

But that's how it was, I guess. Juliet was Mom's. I was Dad's daughter.

I punched, kicked and jabbed until my lungs were screaming and my muscles were weak, and then I cooled down, throwing myself onto the mat once I'd finished stretching. The best thing about working hard enough to physically need the rest was that it stilled my mind and I was thinking about absolutely nothing.

"You're still beating the shit out of these bags, huh?" Juliet asked, stepping down into the musty space and looking over at me.

Despite all the weirdness, it was still nice to see my sister.

"Keeps me in shape," I panted. "Gets my mind to still a bit."

She nodded. "Dad would be happy. Maybe I could use that," she said. She reached out a dainty fist and hit the speed bag, watching it recoil and bounce a bit. Something in the action, and so much in her voice felt sad and lost.

"You doing okay?" I asked her.

She shrugged and punched the heavy bag with her other hand. "Ouch. Shit!" She stared at her knuckles.

"You need to wrap your hands if you're going to hit that hard," I told her, pulling myself to my feet. I switched off my Bluetooth speaker and picked up my water bottle, turning to head back upstairs with my sister, but she stood still. She was staring into the middle distance, unseeing. "Hey, you," I said, bumping shoulders with her. "You sure you're okay?"

A smile flickered over her face and she turned to look at me. "I'm great, Tess. Really." it was the least convincing acting she'd ever done.

"Ryan seems nice." I couldn't help it. There was a strange

excitement in even getting to speak his name, and it didn't seem to matter that I'd told myself I wasn't going to talk about him, think about him today.

I knew it was impossible. He was here. He was gorgeous and kind. And I was no better off than I'd been before my workout, as if speaking his name brought every misplaced feeling I had for him racing right back in.

I tried not to think too hard about the things my sister got to do with him. About whether they'd done any of those things last night after I'd gone to bed, and replayed our single near-kiss over and over in my mind like a lovesick child.

"He's a good guy." The words were right, and she sounded like she meant them, but I'd somehow expected something more. More passion, maybe. More enthusiasm. I knew I'd have a hard time not gushing if Ryan McDonnell was my boyfriend.

"You've just been seeing each other a couple weeks? I mean, you weren't seeing him before … you know …?"

She shook her head as we started up the stairs. "No. I would have been faithful forever. Even though things …" Her voice cracked a bit on the word forever. "Things had gotten harder," she said, and it was as if she'd admitted to killing a kitten. She sounded so guilty, like she blamed herself for failing at marriage.

"Jul," I said, reaching up to pat her back ahead of me. "I'm so sorry."

She turned and gave me an appraising look, and then sighed. "There's so much I want to tell you."

"So tell me." I wasn't used to Juliet being cryptic, but it had been a while since we'd seen one another. Time and space had driven us apart.

"I can't," she said simply, stepping out into the hallway next to the kitchen. "The magazine people are here." She pointed to the front parlor, where I could see people moving past the open doorway and hear unfamiliar voices. One of the hulking security guards stood next to the door and he grinned at Juliet when he saw us standing there. Those guys were creepily everywhere, and managed to stay silent, even though they were huge. I guessed that was their job. I peered around him at the bustle in the room.

"Crap, they're really early," I said, keeping my voice low. It wasn't even nine A.M.

"It's good. Maybe we'll be done early," she said.

"I need to shower. I wanted to be ready. I had a plan." A small panic rose in me. I'd wanted to be prepared for them to arrive, to greet them and offer coffee and tea, to seem worldly and put-together. But they were an hour earlier than I'd expected them, and I was drenched in sweat.

"It's fine Tess, you don't have to wait on anyone." She said it like a person who never worried about waiting on anyone, and the differences between our lives were brought into sharp relief in my mind.

"I got this." I took a deep breath and did what I needed to do. I pretended perspiration wasn't actually dripping from the back of my hair and sliding down my neck as I welcomed the photographers, makeup artists, and the interviewer into my home. I acted like this was how I'd intended to look when the two biggest movie stars in the country were about to be interviewed in my house, like I was just. That. Casual.

"There's some coffee and tea, and some muffins and fruit in the dining room," I told them. "Or, I mean, there will be in a minute or two …"

"I'm sorry we're early," Alison Sands told me, offering the smile I'd seen a few times before when the magazine had done segments on television entertainment shows. She was pretty and put together in her crisp black skirt suit, and standing next to her made me feel even more like a sweaty disaster. "We weren't sure how much time to allow—you're pretty far out here!"

The frown crossed my face before I could contain it. It wasn't as if we lived in the middle of nowhere. Southern Maryland was civilized. We had a Target. And two Starbucks!

"It's fine," I managed, though coming at the time you were invited was much more civilized in my mind than showing up an hour early, especially in the morning. I decided to let it roll off my shoulders, and then I went to defrost muffins I'd made a week ago and brew coffee. Juliet came in to pull some fruit from the refrigerator, maybe sensing my desperation. When we'd gotten it all out on the dining room table and the magazine team was at work setting up for the interview, I turned to my sister.

"I'll be right back," I told her, and then I turned to sprint up the stairs to attempt to break the record for world's quickest shower. Naturally, Ryan was coming down, and I barreled directly into him. Because, clearly, that was how my day was going to go.

"Oh crap," I said, startled as his strong hands found their way around my arms to steady me. "I'm so sorry." He was two steps above me, so I was staring at his chest. His strong, perfect chest, on display through a fitted dark button down shirt. I was already covered in a sheen of sweat, so hopefully he didn't notice the way my skin heated and flushed.

"You okay?" He asked with a laugh in his voice.

"Fine. Sorry." I stepped back down, out of his grip, and dodged around him, in too much of a hurry to try to stifle the careening butterflies in my gut or the desperate desire to stand there in front of him for hours upon hours. Or maybe forever. "Be right back."

I took what could potentially be qualified as a shower in parts of the world where water was scarce—the kind where each part of your body got the vaguest of rinses with the water. Then I put on some makeup and twisted my hair up into a bun, and arrived back downstairs to find the interview already underway. I wondered what kind of notes they might have already made about Juliet's super-sweaty sister.

Juliet and Ryan sat side by side, facing toward the picture window at the front of the parlor. They were flanked by all sorts of lights and reflective umbrellas, and the interviewer sat on a high stool in front of them, her legs crossed primly at the ankles.

"I thought this was a magazine interview," I said to the big dark haired guard standing in the doorway watching.

He turned and gave me a smile that was surprisingly sweet for a guy so huge and terrifyingly … huge. "They're doing this segment for promo and to feature on a couple of the nightly shows."

I nodded as if this was just a standard happening in my daily life, and lingered for just a second. They were still doing sound checks and measuring lighting, so I stepped out and went to the dining room for a cup of coffee and a quick bite.

I was feeling better. I was dressed and dry, and had done hostessy things like making coffee and offering it to the crew. This was more like I'd imagined the day going.

Except. Where was Gran? I didn't hear her cursing, so that was something.

I tiptoed back out of the room and wandered the main level of the house, peeking out onto the porch and scanning the yard. She sometimes did Tai Chi out under the trees on the riverbank, but she wasn't out there now. I approached the door to the room where we'd moved her gaming computer and wasn't too surprised to hear her grumbling at the monitor. I pushed the door open and was greeted by a cloud of dense smoke hanging in the air, its telltale aroma pungent and thick. Because of course Gran wouldn't care what a Hollywood magazine was going to write about us.

"Gran!" I scolded. "It's not even nine AM!"

She turned in her huge black chair and stared at me with

too-round eyes and a little guilty smile. "Tess. I needed to relax. Big raid today."

I shook my head. I did not need this today. "No big raid today. You promised no Warcraft today. And no pot!" I hissed.

"You can't trust anyone over forty," she told me. "Haven't you ever heard that?"

"Oh my God," I said, opening windows and waving my arms around over my head. "It reeks in here. The magazine people are here—do you want them to put this in the article?"

Gran shrugged.

"And now I smell like pot!" So much for appearing put together.

Gran shrugged again, giving me a simpering smile as she crossed her arms.

"No games and no pot until they're gone!" I told her.

"Fine," she said, pouting and then taking another quick drag on her joint.

"Give me that!" I said, reaching to grab it and stub it out in her ashtray.

"You could use it," she said, nodding.

"I'm fine. Just a little …"

"You're all worked up over hotty McHot Stuff being with your sister out there. I remember when you watched that movie of his every day for three weeks."

I had been just slightly obsessed with *Meet me in Manhattan*. But that was a few years ago. I was far more mature now, and Ryan never did romantic movies anymore.

"Gran …" I started, but she reached forward and shut off the monitor, giving me a sweet smile.

"Thank you." I leaned down next to her and gave her a kiss on the cheek. "Maybe you could go sit outside a bit? Get some fresh air?" I worried that the smell of smoke had already wrapped itself through every fiber of her tracksuit, her hair. I didn't know what the magazine people would make of a pot-smoking, Warcraft-raiding granny in Juliet's life, but I had to assume those things wouldn't help paint the picture of her idyllic childhood here in Maryland. We needed to try to help Juliet. She'd been through enough.

Gran finally stood and we went together to the back porch, where I settled her with a muffin, a cup of coffee, and her Kindle. Besides gaming, she had a penchant for erotic literature.

"I'm going back in to watch the interview," I said.

She ignored me, already reading, and I turned quickly, my attention drawn by the sound of a screeching chicken. Oh God. Chessy.

Back inside, Juliet and Ryan sat holding hands casually and smiling as if they did this every day, but Juliet's eyes were huge as she tracked the half-flight, half-sprint of an enraged chicken streaking through the room at Alison.

"Chessy!" I shrieked before I thought better of it. I dashed into the room, pulling the chicken away from where she was trying to peck at the interviewer's legs. Alison had pulled herself up to balance on the top of the stool, her mouth in an exaggerated open gape and her eyes enormous as she stared at me like her last salvation.

"What is that thing?" Alison asked in a whisper-hiss full of the kind of shock that someone who's never been pecked by a house-chicken before will use.

I'd finally caught Chessy and held her against my chest where she quit struggling once she had craned her neck around so she could gaze lovingly at Jack. "This is Chessy," I said, realizing that an insane indoor chicken probably wasn't going to help Juliet. But it was too late to fix this. Better to just be truthful.

"Why is it inside?" Alison asked, horrified.

"She's an indoor chicken," I said, figuring that explaining how Chessy had been targeted by the mean girl chickens out in the coop and bullied within an inch of her little chicken life probably wouldn't be good fodder for the article. "It's very trendy here in Maryland," I said, trying to fix this but realizing I'd already gone too far.

"Really?" Alison asked, finally letting her legs down from where she'd balanced atop the stool.

"Oh yes," I said. "You should see all the fancy ladies out at lunch with their hens in designer bags. I'm surprised they're not doing it in California yet. It's a nod to environmentalism and humane treatment of animals, and antibiotics..." I trailed off, my mind wanting to link fashionable chicken husbandry to global warming somehow, but not quite getting there. I was distracted by the amused smile spreading across Ryan McDonnell's face as he listened to me talk.

His eyes danced and he shook his head lightly, grinning at me.

For a split second, I met his eye and little shocks went through me all the way to my lady bits and back.

"Interesting," Alison was saying as she jotted something in her notebook.

"I'm sorry, I thought Chessy was out of the way," I said, turning to put the chicken back in the kitchen.

"My fault," Jack said, leaning in as I passed him.

Chessy struggled in my arms, every little chicken cell she possessed trying to get closer to Jack.

"I went in the kitchen to put away my coffee cup and she saw me. I thought I got that door closed..."

"A chicken's adoration can unlock any door, I guess," I told him. "Not your fault." I smiled at the big guard who was observing the chicken with wary eyes. He shocked me by reaching out to take her from me.

"I'll just hang on to her." Chessy beamed up at him, nestling her head into his big chest.

"If you're sure," I said. When he didn't protest, but stroked the chicken's head instead, I went back out into the parlor.

Juliet and Ryan were leaning into one another, smiling like a couple that knew every secret the other kept. My stomach twisted as I took up a spot in a corner, out of the way.

"It wasn't love at first sight really," Juliet was saying. "I mean, I'd seen Ryan of course—who hadn't? He was in every amazing action movie I saw." I schooled my face into a mask. I could handle listening to my sister gush about Ryan. Of course I could. He was her boyfriend. To me, he was just … a man I needed to stop thinking about. One who made my whole body feel like it was getting ready to erupt.

Ryan beamed at Juliet. "It was more like complete adoration at first sight," he said, pulling her hand up to kiss.

I stifled a groan. This might be harder to watch than I'd anticipated.

"Are you willing to talk a bit about Zac Stevens? Your divorce and the rumors surrounding it?" The interviewer asked my sister, who stiffened slightly.

"We don't need to drag her through that," Ryan said.

Juliet relaxed a bit. "It's fine. What do you want to know?"

I'd never liked Zac. I wasn't entirely sure Juliet had really liked him. I'd always thought there was something odd about their relationship, but now watching Juliet stiffly holding Ryan's hand, I was beginning to think maybe that's just how my sister was when she was with a man. It was strange, though.

"There are rumors that Zac was caught cheating with one of the staff at your house, Juliet. Is that accurate?" I already knew this was true. I hated that my sister had to deal with that.

Juliet nodded. "Unfortunately, yes."

"And it was you who caught them?"

"Again, yes. Not my favorite way to return home after being on location for weeks." She tried a smile, but it faltered. I'd already heard the whole story, and I hated it. Poor Juliet.

Ryan reached out his other hand and laid it atop Juliet's, cradling her hand between his. She shot him a grateful smile. He was sweet, caring.

"There are other rumors," the reporter continued. "About the settlement. That you're being blackmailed, that Zac has a tape he's threatening to release."

I felt shock work its way through me. Was this what Juliet had wanted to tell me? Was Zac really enough of a dick to be trying to blackmail the woman who made him famous and gave him a life he never would have had on his own?

Juliet forced a tight smile to her lips. "That is something I can't discuss, actually," she said. "The settlement is still being sorted by the lawyers, so I'm not able to give you any specifics, I'm afraid."

"But what about the blackmail rumor?" The reporter persisted.

Ryan leaned forward, gave the reporter a smile that made my blood heat. "I think we can find other things to talk about, can't we? No one in the midst of a divorce wants their dirty laundry aired. Not even America's sweetheart." His words said, "back off, lady," but his tone and his smile almost made me believe he'd invited the reporter home for Christmas, they were so charming.

She stilled, swallowing a frown, and then moved on to asking about the movie Ryan and Juliet had just finished working on. I listened, but found myself more and more distracted just watching Ryan. The way his long legs stretched out before him, clad in dark jeans that showed the contours of the muscles beneath, the easy set of his torso in the chair. His clean-shaven face and the azure blue eyes surrounded by all those dark lashes gave him an aura of sincerity, of good-natured strength that drew me in. And his voice was gravel laced with honey; every time he spoke, something inside me stood to attention, urged me to move closer.

At one point I met his eyes over the head of the interviewer and my entire body zinged with a jolt of vibrating fire. I'd tried to avoid looking right at him, but when his gaze met mine, he held it for a long minute. And when he dropped my eyes and turned back to my sister, I was left feeling cold. This was not good.

As the first portion of the interview wrapped up and the threesome stood and made to move through the house for photos in various places, I felt like I was rousing myself from sleep. I'd been watching Ryan so intensely, given the ability to do so by the setup of the interview and the situation. And I'd been watching my sister, too—watching them together. It was like picking at a painful wound, but I couldn't help it.

The reporter spotted me as they moved from the room. "So," she said. "Thanks for setting everything up for us, Tess. And for handling the runaway chicken situation."

"It's no trouble," I lied. It was a fair amount of trouble, and given that we were expecting about a hundred guests tomorrow evening for Gran's ninetieth birthday party, I had a lot of other things I could be doing.

"So nice of you to let us invade like this." She looked thoughtful. "Would you be willing to be in a few photos? Janet can touch up your makeup a bit." She indicated a girl seated next to an open case, brushes and powders on the table before her.

I eyed Janet and her array of tools. Makeup had never been my forte. I'd dashed through the shower this morning and then put on a little blush and mascara before swiping a gloss on my lips and coming down.

"Um. Sure," I said. A tiny part of me thrilled at getting to stick a toe into the world where my sister lived. But another part of me wondered why I would bother. This wasn't my thing at all. My world was kayaks and paddles, water, sunscreen, and bug spray.

The reporter grinned and nodded once at Janet, who waved me to her table, where she proceeded to douse me in powders and creams, pulling my hair from its clip and waving a blow dryer around me. A half hour later, I joined Gran on the back porch, where she was expounding on the history of our plantation. She particularly liked the less glamorous parts.

"What most people wouldn't probably know about Tobias Walthen," she was saying, "was that he was a man of great appetites, if you get my drift."

The assembled crewmembers shrugged and shook their heads. They were not getting her drift. Jack patted Chessy as he listened to Gran.

"Well, he had four different wives at one point, but he was a nice guy, see? When Thomas Jefferson came down this way, staying at this very house while he picked up some tips on growing tobacco and cannabis back at his own place in Virginia, Tobias offered to share."

"Share his ..." One of the cameramen said.

"His women!" Gran confirmed, her voice shrill with delight. "And then there was the time Alexander Hamilton—"

"That's probably enough history," I said, giving Gran a meaningful look.

She shrugged and returned to her book, muttering about people getting all worked up about nothing. I took a seat at the table, and gazed out over the lawn. One of the photographers was standing near Ryan and Juliet, posing them in front of a huge old tree. Juliet was smiling at the camera. Ryan's heated gaze, however, was focused on me.

CHAPTER NINE
RYAN

Tess wasn't the kind of woman who needed makeup to look better. She was gorgeous in every incarnation I'd seen so far—when she'd stood uncertainly on the steps as we'd arrived, sweating out in the barn from moving tables and chairs, and covered in perspiration and dressed in workout gear when she'd nearly knocked me over on the stairs. Every time I saw her it felt like seeing her again for the first time, like some kind of epic revelation my brain couldn't hang on to. But seeing her out on the porch after Janet finished touching up her makeup and hair … I'd honestly never been more attracted to anyone.

We stood just off the porch, and I looked up at her in amazement. Her dark hair cascaded around her gorgeous pale face, hanging in loose waves over her shoulders and down her back. Her skin glowed from within, the lightest blush touching her pale cheeks. And her eyes—always compelling and deep—had become endless pools of light, reflecting the mid-morning sun in the green and brown depths.

"Ryan," the photographer called, and I snapped my head around to see Juliet and the camera crew standing on the grass waiting for me to follow. I'd been literally stunned still by Tess's appearance, and realized much too late that I'd been staring.

Tess gave me a smile, one that seemed to say, "okay, creeper, move along," and I came back to myself. I was never going to sell how into Juliet I was if I kept drooling over her sister. I jogged across the lawn to Juliet, each step away from Tess feeling so wrong it hurt.

"Tess, will you join us?" the reporter, Alison Sands, called to her. "And we need a few shots with your grandmother, too."

I slipped an arm around Juliet's waist, more conscious than ever that I was in danger of ruining the deception, that my hammering heart and distracted mind might give us away if anyone had the slightest reason to suspect Juliet wasn't the cause of them. I didn't turn to watch Tess approach, but I could fucking feel her draw near as we turned to look out toward the water.

"Hey, babe," Juliet said, leaning into my side. Right. Juliet. Focus on Juliet. I owed her my best performance.

Alison grinned at us. "What a cute couple," she said. "Would you guys be up for some sexier shots? I saw the airport footage and it's trending so well online. I think people are up for seeing more of that intimacy between you." She waved us toward the edge of the lawn, where it sloped down into sand at the edge of the river.

"Sure," I said, still feeling a tether pulling my focus backward, where I knew Tess was just feet from me.

"Tess, why don't you jump in here for now? We'll get a few shots of you with the couple and the big house in the background, a few with Helen, and then a couple of the water. And then we'll get to the sexy stuff."

Tess let out a laugh that sounded uncomfortable, and it worked its way inside me. This had to be strange for her, having this odd interruption to her daily life, having these people here. I glanced at the enormous security guys who stood on the periphery, constantly vigilant on her sister's behalf. The bigger one—Jace, I think his name was?—looked extremely unhappy as he stared at my arm around Juliet's waist. I wondered for a brief moment if she might need to worry about her bodyguard turning obsessive. I'd heard stories about things like that. But Juliet had hired the best, she'd told me so when I'd mentioned the guys who'd been accompanying us everywhere since I'd met her in the town car to begin our charade.

The photographer arranged us, Juliet in the circle of my arms and Tess standing at her side, and we shot for what felt like hours, eventually adding Gran to the mix too. I hoped the shots were good, but I couldn't stop thinking about how I had the wrong woman in my arms.

We moved around the property a bit, posing here and there, always me with Juliet, Tess on the side, and eventually, Gran seated in front of us, complaining loudly and plucking at the dress Tess had made her go change into. "This is why I only wear cotton," she said. "Preferably Juicy Couture. Doesn't bind. Plenty of give."

Alison was scribbling furiously.

"You don't need to include that," Tess said, laughing. "Just pretend she's being gracious and acting like any other ninety year old woman."

"Damn it, you people!" Gran spit out. "I'm not ninety until tomorrow. For now, I'm fifty-nine, just like I have been for years."

Gran lightened the mood, but it all felt so false to me. Still, nothing was worse than when Tess stood behind the photographer watching us as Juliet and I were directed to lay down in the grass with the water behind us. If only I did have the hots for Juliet, it would have been a dream come true—staking my claim publicly for all of America to see. Instead, it felt like the worst acting I'd ever done.

They took shots of her straddling me, her hair cascading down around us as she sat with her long legs bent on either side of my hips and I reached up, holding her. They took shots of me hovering over her, as if we were close to losing control and going for it right here on the ground with everyone around. They pushed us to be closer, to make it sexier, and they even got a few shots with Juliet's leg up around my hip and my hand on her breast. It was veering out of PG territory, and I tried as hard as I could not to look at Tess, but it was impossible, especially with Gran at her side, occasionally heckling things like, "Get it, son!"

Tess was beautiful, even as she watched Juliet and me together. Her eyes burned and her skin flushed, and I wondered if she felt it too—this strange connection between us. I barely knew her, so why did I feel like I was betraying her somehow, out here touching her sister for the camera? She was practically a stranger, but I knew I couldn't watch her rolling around on the ground with another man. It would potentially kill me. And Tess's body language and darting eyes told me it wasn't comfortable for her either. Or was I reading into the way her breath seemed to lift her chest in shallow breaths, the high red dots in her cheeks?

"I think we've got what we need for now," Alison said finally. Relief washed through me and I practically leapt away from Juliet before remembering myself and stepping back a bit.

We thanked the crew and they packed up and headed for the van out front while we headed back to the house.

"I'll get some lunch put together," Tess said tightly over her shoulder, and then she disappeared into the house, leaving Juliet and me on the front step.

"I think that went really well," Juliet said, stepping away from me and glancing nervously at the security guard who stood at the edge of the porch. She probably worried he might overhear us—I assumed even her security detail didn't know we were just pretending, though they must have been confused by my sudden appearance at Juliet's side. They had to know I hadn't been around the house prior to this trip, that we hadn't needed them to check restaurants or hold off photographers around town at home. I pulled her farther down the long porch to a set of chairs, and we sat down.

"I think we should tell your sister," I said. I hadn't even planned to say it, but the feeling that I was lying to Tess was eating at me. Which made no sense, given that she was basically a stranger. But there it was. I wanted her to know, needed her to know that I wasn't interested in Juliet.

Juliet's eyebrows flew up and she widened her eyes at me. "I don't know," she said. "The more people believing we're a couple, the better."

"It's just hard to keep it all up inside the house," I said. "And she already knows we are sleeping in separate rooms. And the interview's over."

"That's true," she said, one finger at the edge of her lips. She lifted a shoulder in a half shrug. "The reporters are coming back for the party, but I guess we can tell Tess. We'd better not tell Gran, though. You never know what she'll say."

"Gran seems pretty harmless," I said, my heart swelling at the idea of telling Tess the truth and my head spinning with the possibility of telling her other things.

"Gran is many things. She's not harmless, though." Juliet looked wary and I wondered how dangerous a little old lady could really be. Though hearing her yell "go for it, Jules!" as we were instructed to grope one another on the lawn made me think maybe Juliet had a point.

When Tess came out to get us for lunch, I followed the sisters through the house, waiting for Juliet to say the words that would free me, to tell Tess what I needed her to know. I'd offered to tell her, but Juliet had looked at me like I was crazy. Of course it would be her place to tell her.

Lunch was quiet—everyone gazing out over the rolling green lawn and staying inside their own heads. Every time Juliet opened her mouth I hoped it would be to let the cat out of the bag, and my heart would climb just a bit up my throat. But she didn't broach the topic.

We cleaned our dishes up, Tess avoiding my eye the entire time as I struggled with my desire to just blurt the truth.

It wasn't my truth to tell her though. Juliet had been clear about that. They were sisters. I was the outsider.

CHAPTER TEN

TESS

Watching Ryan and Juliet take sexy photos on the bank of the river was a challenge. I'd lived my life watching my sister get pretty much everything she wanted—or at least getting the things most people seemed to want. And watching her with Ryan was like grinding salt into recently opened old wounds that I'd been sure were healed over.

Which I was aware was one hundred percent ridiculous.

Ryan was a movie star I'd just met. He and my sister were together. And for good reason—she was perfect. She was gorgeous and thin, funny and charming. Standing next to her had always made it pretty clear who got the good-looks genes in our family.

Still, it wasn't like I had a self-esteem problem. I'd always been happy with myself. I looked just like our mother, so how could that ever be a bad thing? My mother had been soft and sweet, with her long dark hair and her wide light eyes. I missed her, and if I got to see her again when I looked into the mirror in some small way, I was happy about that.

Still, I needed to remember I wasn't a movie star. And I

didn't date them. Soon they'd be back on a plane to Hollywood and this would all be just a memory. I needed to focus on that. On my life here. On me, Gran, my business.

The strange intimacy that had sprung up between Ryan and me was compelling, but I had to keep telling myself it didn't mean anything.

And that became easier as I went in and pulled lunch together. My phone chimed on the counter with a text, and I moved to pick it up.

Gran. Who had raced to her gaming room as soon as the interviewers had left. Evidently she'd scanned the news before she logged onto her game, because she'd sent me a link along with about thirty emojis of everything from camels to little faces with hearts all around them, and even a few pretty vulgar emojis I didn't even know existed.

I was considering revoking her phone privileges.

I pulled up the link. It was the video I'd seen just before Juliet arrived, and as much as I dreaded watching it again, I couldn't help it.

The video began, and there were my sister and Ryan at LAX, making out like teenagers. She looked completely enraptured with the kiss, and then his hand slipped to her breast and my stomach turned. I switched off the phone, shoving it into my back pocket and turning back to the counter with my heart in my throat. Why the hell did I care?

"Hey." Juliet stepped in through the swinging back door after we'd finished lunch. "Can I talk to you?"

I didn't want to look at her. It was immature and silly, but I was feeling angry with her, angry for being Juliet. For being gorgeous, for being famous. And I knew that was unfair but it was an old jealousy. Maybe it was in my DNA. I took a deep breath, reminding myself that this was my sister. I loved her. And I didn't see her enough. "Sure." My voice wasn't as friendly as I'd intended it to be.

"Are you okay?" She stepped closer, dipping her head to catch my gaze.

I pasted on a smile. "Fine. What's up?"

"Uh, well … It feels wrong misleading you," she began.

I felt my forehead wrinkle. Misleading me? I knew there was something she was hiding. Was she going to tell me about the blackmail rumor? About whatever had her staring off into space distractedly? "What?"

"Ryan and I agreed that we should tell you the truth."

Oh God. I braced myself. What did she mean? Were they pregnant? Had they eloped or something? I had no idea what she could be about to say. "Okay," I said, my voice barely a whisper.

"We aren't really together." The words hung in the air between us while I tried to sort through them and force them to make sense. I'd just watched a video in which they were very much together.

In which his hand and her breast were definitely together.

Where their lips were so together it was stomach-turning.

I stared at her, open-mouthed. They'd been rolling around on the lawn just moments before, the photographer telling them how in love they looked, how sexy the shots were. "What?"

"We're faking it. As a distraction for the press."

What? I shook my head slowly, letting the words process. Confusion and relief chased each other through my mind and words flitted away, lost to the murk in my mind. Luckily, Juliet kept talking so I didn't have to.

"Zac is blackmailing me with a video he has of us. A sex tape. He's saying if I don't agree to his divorce terms, then he'll release it. My lawyers are working on it, but I've pretty much told them to go ahead and give him whatever he wants. The press has been all over it, talking about my shitty deal and looking for reasons why I'd agree to it. I needed a distraction. I needed something for them to focus on besides the complete train wreck that was my marriage."

"Oh." I tried to find other words to say, but my mind was spinning around all the information she'd just given me. My first reaction was to be hurt that she'd treated me just like the press—lied to me as if I wasn't part of the inner circle, couldn't be trusted. Then again, she was telling me now. And the strange complicated life my sister led was what made her feel she needed to lie to me.

"I could never live in your world," I told her. It was true. That any of this made rational sense to her was beyond me. I could never handle having to make choices like these, having to pick which aspect of my life I wanted splashed all over the tabloids.

She winced slightly, but she brushed off my comment with a little shrug. "I needed someone to help me, and Ryan is a good guy. We worked on that movie together and I knew he might need ..." she trailed off and pulled her bottom lip between her teeth. "I knew he could use the lift. It was my agent's idea, really."

"The lift?"

"His career's been flagging. His last couple movies didn't do well. He was slipping."

"And being linked romantically to you will help him?"

She had the grace to blush, but she nodded confirmation. "My agent thinks she can get him onto the next film I'm doing—it's a romantic suspense and they want an action lead for the romantic hero. We kind of made a deal."

"He acts like he loves you and you get him the job that will make him a star?" I understood the idea fundamentally, but I hadn't decided yet if it was just business, or if there was some kind of moral deficit in someone who might make a deal like that.

She sighed. "Basically. It's just business."

So Juliet didn't see any moralistic side to the deal. She wasn't worried about it beyond whatever specifics they'd agreed upon. Maybe it really wasn't my business either.

"Man," I breathed. Could the rules that governed behavior in Hollywood really be so different than those in the rest of the world? Still, I didn't really blame my sister. She understood her world—that was how she'd gotten to the top. But I hated the idea of career success being based on manipulating other people's feelings. Mine included. I was disappointed in her, and I was trying to figure out if I had any right to feel that way. I wasn't in her shoes—in her life. "Okay," I said. "Well, thanks for telling me, I guess."

"Ryan didn't want to lie to you." She squeezed my arm and smiled. "And neither did I." Juliet turned and headed back outside, leaving me standing there, reeling.

Ryan didn't want to lie to you.

The power those last words had over me was frightening, and they left me shaking slightly as I repeated them in my head. Why did Ryan care what I thought? Ryan was a movie star. He was a guy who went around flirting with and touching anyone he liked because he knew the power he had over people. He was a guy who'd link himself to a starlet in a false sexual relationship just to get ahead. Didn't that make him kind of a dirty asshole? Or was it like Juliet said—was he a nice guy? In a world where the rules were so very different, was that the kind of thing nice guys did?

Ryan didn't want to lie to you.

Most importantly, why did Ryan feel like I needed to know the truth?

I was confused and a little bit angry. But down deep inside me, in a place I was trying hard not to think about, a flame had been lit. A little flame glowed and stirred as I considered this idea. Ryan wasn't with my sister. Ryan had almost kissed me. Ryan had asked her to tell me the truth.

The little flame burned brighter, and I realized with horror that it was a flame of hope.

CHAPTER ELEVEN
RYAN

When lunch was over, I stepped off the sweeping back porch, gazing out at the river lapping at the beach down below and the huge old trees leaning over the wide yard, cooling the still air. This place felt magical to me—part of it must have been the knowledge that it had been here for hundreds of years, it had seen turning points in American history that I'd read about in books. And, if Gran was to be believed, plenty of history I hadn't read about. Who knew the founding fathers were such stone cold players?

When you've lived your entire life on the West Coast, this kind of real history makes an impression. Even the air here gave the sense of calm steadiness, of patience, as if the whole place was saying, *I've been here this long, I'll be here forever.* It made me feel small, somehow, less solid. But it also made me aware of the impermanence of my own life—not that my own history hadn't done a pretty good job of that. But it just hammered home the knowledge that our time here was short.

And while the history of the place was definitely interesting, it was the present that held my interest most.

I didn't know what it was about Tess, or what might exist

between us if we gave it a chance, but it was something I'd never felt before.

I turned back to the house, and could see Tess through the kitchen window at the sink. Juliet had gone inside with her after lunch, winking at me as she'd gone, so I was pretty sure by now Tess knew the truth. I was less sure what that meant for me. Would she be angry that we'd lied to her? Would she think I was just another dirty Hollywood type, doing anything to get ahead?

Wasn't I?

I thought about Dad, back in Los Angeles, about the money it took to take care of him. I thought about the abandoned plans I'd had once for a completely different kind of life. And I thought about the deal I'd made with Juliet when the roles seemed to be drying up and the money with them. I'd had a reason for what I'd done—maybe Tess would understand.

I crossed the wide porch, ignoring the squawk of Chessy, who was chasing Jack across the lawn as he hovered just far enough away from me that I knew he was assigned to me for today, and I went inside to find Tess.

"Hey," I said, stepping into the kitchen. She was wiping the countertop, cleaning things up after lunch.

She stopped moving and looked up to meet my eye, something quizzical and uncertain there. "Hey," she said, and then opened the dishwasher and put a few things into the rack.

I leaned against the counter, watching her. I wanted to talk to her, but if I was being honest, I just liked watching her move. She was lithe and graceful, but she wasn't lean like her sister. Tess was clearly a woman, with curves under her clothes that begged for exploration, and a hint of movement when she walked that was mesmerizing. I'd never had a type, I didn't think, but my hands itched to fill themselves with those generous curves, and I was beginning to think I'd been living in a world surrounded by women who were definitely not my type.

"You're making me nervous," Tess said, finally stopping her movements around the kitchen and turning to face me. "Staring like that."

"Sorry," I said, brushing my hands against my thighs as if I could clear the nervous energy out of my body. "Is there anything I can help with today?" I tried. "For the party?"

Tess washed her hands slowly and seemed to think about her answer. "I took today off work so I could get things ready for Gran's party, but I think things are pretty much set. Turns out I'm more organized than even I realized." Her light laugh dissipated some of the nerves that were gathering in my stomach.

She ran a hand over her hair, smoothing up a tendril that had escaped over her shoulder and was hanging in her face. She looked at me a long minute, and little spikes of excitement skewered my gut, my muscles tightening as I tried to figure out what the look in her eyes meant.

"I'm sorry we lied," I said. I wanted to banish the awkwardness between us, address the biggest issue so maybe we could move forward.

She nodded slowly, lowering her eyes and spreading her hands on the countertop, her slim fingers splaying wide on the dark granite. "Yeah," she said, her voice almost a breath. "I get it. I mean, I guess I do." She turned to face me, her beautiful face bunched with worry. "You and Juliet … you live these lives I can't even begin to understand. Your world is just so different." She smiled and shook her head as if to brush away her concerns.

"Not that different," I said.

She squinted up at me, like she was trying to see inside me somehow, see why I would agree to lie. "It's okay," she said finally.

The topic seemed to be closed, even though there was a lot more I wanted to tell her. Maybe now, standing in her kitchen with an insane chicken shrieking just outside the door, wasn't the right time. I hoped there would be more time for us. That she might give me a chance.

"Tess," I said, lowering my voice and taking a step nearer. "I'd love to see more of the area. I wondered if you'd have time to show me around a little bit while I'm here."

Her eyes widened and her breath hitched, making her gorgeous chest swell before she let out a quick huff of breath. "I mean ... the party is tomorrow night, and ..."

"So let me help you get ready. What can I do?"

"I mean ... I guess it's mostly done, really. The cake is done. The caterers will do the rest."

"So do you have some time?" I should have stayed back, let her tell me she didn't want anything to do with me, let her tell me that because I'd lied, whatever magnetic pull was between us meant nothing. But I couldn't. I needed to see if she felt it too, now that I was free to try. I stepped closer still, until we were just six inches apart. I could feel the heat of her body against my own, and longed to close the distance, to pull her into my arms. "Please show me around," I said, my voice low.

Her eyes didn't leave mine, and I saw it the second she gave in, her body relaxing slightly. Relief washed through me. "Sure," she said on a whispered sigh. "Okay."

"Great," I said, trying to push down the excitement building in my veins at the idea of a day spent at Tess's side. "I'll get ready."

"Sure," she said again, looking a little baffled as she shook her head lightly. "Okay. Fifteen minutes?"

"Perfect." I was about to start for the stairs to get ready when Juliet walked in, spotted us inches from one another, and stopped in her tracks. "Everything okay in here?" Her nose wrinkled and she cocked her head to the side, trying to decipher the odd atmosphere, mistaking intimacy for trouble.

Tess turned back to the sink and rinsed her hands again. "Just planning for an afternoon of sightseeing. You in?"

I didn't want Juliet to say yes, but schooled my expression into something friendly.

Juliet laughed lightly, but glanced over her shoulder back at the porch before responding. "I think I'll pass. I've seen it all. Plus ... if I go, we might get mobbed. Do you mind showing Ryan around on your own?"

I ignored the unspoken assertion that I was not so famous we'd get mobbed, mostly because my heart was busy swelling in my chest and my stomach had just filled with little trapeze artists at the thought of having Tess all to myself for the afternoon.

"Yeah, that's fine," Tess said.

"I'll look after Granny." Juliet said. "You don't mind, do you Ryan?"

Mind? I was trying to hide how very much I did not mind. "Not at all," I said. "It'll give me a chance to get to know your sister a bit better and see a little more of Maryland."

That strange look passed over Juliet's face again, as if someone wanting to get to know Tess was actually a little confusing. But she covered it quickly with a smile. "Great."

Fifteen minutes later, I stood on the front porch waiting for Tess. The front door opened, and Granny stepped out lightly, and gave me a direct look, one eyebrow raised. She wasn't holding a shotgun or anything, but her look made it clear she had something to say to me. When the door swung shut behind her, she faced me, her thin arms crossed over her narrow chest, the pale dress she'd worn for the photos looking incongruous in place of her usual track suit.

"Tess says you two are going out for some sightseeing."

"Yes ma'am."

"Don't fuck with my granddaughter," she said plainly.

Shock trickled through my chest like ice water. "Uh, no ma'am."

"Don't 'no ma'am' me. I know your type," she said, pointing a bony finger at me. "Too big for your britches, full of yourself, maybe. Good-looking guy like you ... well, you need to know that Tess is strong and smart and happy, just the way she is. And if you screw any of that up, you'll have me to answer to."

I wasn't quite sure where this was coming from, but I tried to accept the warning and reassure this fierce old woman that I had no intention of hurting either of her granddaughters—not if I could help it. She still believed I was dating Juliet, as far as I knew. "Both of your granddaughters are incredible," I told her. "I'm lucky to know them both."

She eyed me then, crossing her arms again. "Well, you'll have to pick one," she said, and then turned on her heel and went back into the house.

Gran was just being protective, and I thought both Tess and Juliet were lucky to have her looking out for them. I didn't want to hurt anyone, and I hoped I could get to know Tess and try to make my heart happy while keeping my agreement with Juliet—hopefully making both of our careers better.

I tried to shake the tension from my shoulders, swinging my arms as I waited for Tess, who appeared a minute later. Her hair was pulled back again, as it had been this morning, but now it was swinging behind her in a ponytail, with just a few tendrils around her face. She'd removed some of the makeup from earlier, and her cheeks glowed pink beneath those luminous eyes. My nerves stirred up again at the sight of her, my stomach flipping when she smiled at me. "Ready?" she asked.

"Definitely," I said. I wanted to add something about how amazing she looked, how happy I was to get to spend some time alone with her, but I wasn't sure I was completely off the hook for lying to her in the first place about Juliet. I decided to just be a good sightseer, go along for the ride and find out if the potential I felt could be something real.

"Did Granny say something awful to you?" She looked back toward the door.

"Not at all. She was just warning me that if I fuck with you she'll kill me." I followed Tess down the stairs to the driveway. She spun to look at me again, widening her eyes.

"Seriously?"

I lifted a shoulder in a half-shrug. "It's good to have someone looking out for you," I told her.

"Hey," she said. "Do we need to take one of those guys with us?" She angled her head toward where Jack was standing, holding the chicken to his chest.

I shook my head. "They're Juliet's. I don't need them and they don't work for me anyway." I lifted a hand to Jack. "Be back in a bit!"

He waved at me and Chessy let out a squawk. I heard him shushing her as I followed Tess.

As we walked toward the garage, which was a three-bay building set apart from the house, I dropped a hand lightly on Tess's lower back, keeping pace by her side. She stiffened at the contact at first, and I remembered too late that she'd asked me not to touch her. I took my hand away, whispering, "Sorry."

Tess shot a glance up at me, as if trying to read my intention in my eyes. "It's okay," she said, and I hoped she could see some part of the way I might feel about her on my face. The gesture had been natural, almost protective.

We climbed into her mini Cooper and she maneuvered us out of the garage and down the long driveway between the fields. I fought the urge to touch her again, but admired the way her leg flexed and moved as she drove, her muscles stretching the dark denim. Soon we were trundling down curving country roads, huge green trees leaning toward us from either side. The sides of the road were shadowy and dark, a dense verdant wood stretching out on either side of us, twisting with vines and low brush. "It's so different from California," I said, thinking aloud.

"Yeah?" Tess asked, smiling.

"You've never been?" Surprise lifted my voice. I'd have thought she would have visited her sister at some point. I liked the idea that maybe someday I could be the one to show her California for the first time.

"Nah. That's Juliet's thing. I'm happy here." It was a simple statement, and I turned to see Tess's face glow as she said it. "This is home," she added.

I nodded, wishing I knew what that meant. Home. I understood the idea, the concept. I'd just never really had a home myself, never felt like I belonged anywhere enough to stay. "Must be nice," I said.

"What?" Tess asked, swinging her gaze to mine and then finding the road again.

"Feeling so at home that you don't want to leave," I said. "I don't think I've ever had that."

"Where did you grow up?"

"Out west. My dad traveled for work and got assigned to new territories a lot. We lived in Colorado, Nevada, New Mexico and Texas for a while. A little time in California. That was when I ran away." This wasn't something I shared with a lot of people. I let the information out and watched for her reaction.

Surprise lifted her brows and turned her mouth into a tiny circle. "Ran away?"

"I didn't want to move again."

"But your family …?"

"It was just me and Dad by then. Mom got tired of moving a long time before. I called her first, to see if I could live with her. She stayed in Nevada …" I trailed off. I hadn't really intended to get into all this today, but it felt so natural to share it with Tess. I wanted her to know me, even the parts of me that weren't glamorous and clean.

"But ...?" Tess looked at me.

I forced my voice to sound light. "She figured she was all done parenting by then, I guess." I swallowed hard, keeping the smile on my face. I stared out the window for a minute, remembering the hard finality in my mother's words when she'd told me that she didn't want me. It still hurt, tearing something inside me every time I thought of it. I sucked in a breath, and was thankful when I felt the air shift as Tess readied another question.

"So why are you doing it?" The question came out harsh, and Tess turned her head, glaring at me for a brief moment before turning back to look out at the road.

"Doing ...?"

"Pretending to date my sister."

I knew I'd have to explain myself at some point. Might as well get it out of the way. "It was her agent's idea. I had a small role in the last film she did and there was chemistry. On screen, at least. The media liked it and some false rumors got started. Her agent thought we could capitalize on those and try to keep the sharks fed so they won't go sniffing around where they shouldn't."

"You mean the divorce."

"Right."

"What's in it for you, though?" She sounded less accusatory now, and I felt my nerves unspool a little bit.

"A part in her next film as the romantic lead, mostly. A career boost. A chance to be as successful as I've always thought I wanted to be." It was the story I'd told myself over and over. But no matter how famous I'd gotten so far, it didn't seem to change much. People knowing who you were wasn't the same as someone really knowing you. I was nowhere near as famous as Juliet, but the little taste I'd gotten so far tasted a lot like loneliness.

And the real answer wasn't that I wanted success. It was that I needed money. Enough money that my dad could live someplace where he'd be safe and taken care of. Someplace nice.

Tess seemed to be satisfied with my half-answer, and she drove in silence now. I watched the dense woods fly by either side of the car, wishing I could bring her smile back.

"Any Sasquatch sightings down here?" I asked. "I can totally imagine catching a glimpse of him running through these dense woods."

Tess's laughter was sweet and honest, a sound that made my cells feel lighter, effervescent. "I don't think so," she said. "Though there is a car I see sometimes that's all painted with camouflage and says something like 'Sasquatch Response Team.' I stood behind the guy who drives it at the grocery store once, and he told the clerk all about his important 'work' and gave her a card. When he'd left, she showed it to me. He's a Sasquatch Specialist."

"Oh my God, that's amazing," I said, wishing I could meet the guy. "And they say we get all the kooks in California."

Tess pulled into a long paved driveway between the tall trees, and we passed a little tollbooth, where she paid a few dollars, though there was no one inside.

"Where are we?" I asked.

"Point Lookout State Park," she said. "It's a state park right on the tip of the peninsula. A lot of people come down here to camp or hike or picnic. This was a civil war prison camp." She said this the way most people announced that we'd be getting ice cream.

"Exciting," I said, my tone mocking her slightly. Though the idea of a prison camp did not sound at all romantic or like a good place to get to know someone, the scenery was actually beautiful. There were few other cars in the parking lot, and no one in sight. The birds were calling to one another from the treetops, and I could smell the salt of the ocean.

She sniffed as she parked the car. "It is pretty exciting," she told me. "And if you can't appreciate Maryland's history, this is gonna be a long day for you. I've got plans to show you the state's first capital and about sixteen different churches all built before California was even a state."

I loved the edge of teasing in her voice, her clear fascination with her home state.

Tess led me on a tour of the park, pointing out where a civil war hospital once stood, and ushering me around the site of a prisoner-of-war camp where the Union held Confederate soldiers through the last years of the war.

"It had to be horrible for them," Tess said, looking out over the water that surrounded the tip of the peninsula where the park was situated. "That's Virginia right across the Potomac. If they could just get there, they'd be home, safe in Confederate territory."

"Quite a swim," I said, gazing across the wide river but finding my eyes drawn back to the woman beside me. "I bet some tried it though." I wandered around a bit, sweating in the dense close air of the woods, glad for the occasional breeze off the water. "Wait a minute. Wasn't Maryland part of the Confederacy? You're south of the Mason Dixon."

"Switched sides," Tess said, gesturing for me to follow her back to the trail. We walked in silence for a moment then, picking our way along beneath arching branches and over the slightly muddy path. I walked behind her, unable to keep my eyes from following the sway of her hips in her jeans, the way her ponytail seemed to bob in time with her steps.

I was just about to step a bit closer, try to find words to tell her how happy I was to have a day with her, a chance to get to know her, to explore this feeling I had around her, when a family appeared on the trail in front of us.

A man and a woman were leading two bored-looking teenagers around the park, and I shot them a smile as they were about to pass us. The teenaged girl was just stepping past me when she glanced up, and her face went from bored to excited in a split second, her mouth opening and her eyes going wide.

"Oh my God," she said. Then she squealed, and turned to her mother, grabbing her hand. "Mom! It's Ryan McDonnell." She turned back to me. "You're Ryan McDonnell!"

I was rarely recognized these days, and Maryland was the last place I'd expected someone to know me. Surprise and a hint of embarrassment washed through me, and I felt the color rise in my neck. "I am," I said. "Or was, last I checked."

Tess stepped slightly away as the family bunched closer together, staring and smiling.

"Can I take a selfie?" The girl asked, holding out her phone.

"Sure," I laughed, shooting Tess a quick look. She stood to one side, looking amused.

The girl moved in close and I leaned in over her shoulder as she took the picture, and then the woman pulled something out of her purse. "Will you sign this?" she asked, handing me a pen.

"Of course," I said. As I signed my name on an envelope for the lady, her husband found his voice. "That last movie you made, the one in Antarctica? With the zombies?"

I cringed and braced myself for him to tell me how awful it was. I knew how terrible it was, but it hurt any time someone agreed with the critics' assessment, and for some reason I didn't want him to say it in front of Tess. "Yeah?"

"I loved that movie, man." The guy grinned at me and

slapped me on the back. "Don't listen to those Hollywood jerks man, you're good. Really good."

Now my blush grew hotter. I was definitely not used to praise from unexpected places. "Wow, thank you. That really means a lot to me." It did. It was almost embarrassing how much.

"You're awesome, dude," the other kid said, maybe feeling left out.

The mother looked at Tess suddenly, as if realizing for the first time I wasn't here alone, just waiting for them to find me in the woods. "Oh, guys. We're interrupting. Sorry," she said to Tess. "We'll let you get on with your day. Come on," she said, gathering her family together again. "So nice to meet you. Have a good visit."

The teenaged girl followed her mother, but kept glancing back over her shoulder and smiling, and finally waved at us as they disappeared around a stand of thick trees.

I turned to Tess, stuffing my hands in my pockets and hoping it hadn't ruined whatever might have been building between us so far.

"You were so nice to them," Tess said, smiling at me. "That was really good of you. I bet you made that girl's year. Her mom's too." She stepped back to my side, closer than she'd been before, and we continued walking in the direction the family had come from. "Does that happen a lot?"

"No," I said. "Not like with your sister. I can still stay under the radar most of the time. Especially lately."

"Does it bother you? Do you wish you were more famous?" She looked up at me over her shoulder, her brows wrinkling as she posed the question. I wanted to make her smile again, make the line ease away.

"Not really," I said. "Honestly, I'd rather have the anonymity, but fame does kind of equal success, and I don't think anyone starts out at something and doesn't wish to be successful."

She bobbed her head. "Fair point. So it's kind of a tradeoff. Your privacy for money and good roles."

"I guess so. The money is really the key thing, unfortunately. But I kind of hope I can save enough to take care of the things I need to take care of, and then maybe do something else." I thought about my dad, stopping myself from wishing things were different. He was family—the only I had—and it was my responsibility to take care of him.

"Something else, huh? Like what?"

"I used to think I might open a restaurant," I said, feeling like I was making a confession of sorts. I didn't talk about it often, but I missed the quiet meditation working in the kitchen had always brought me.

"A restaurant?" Tess was smiling up at me, almost leaning into my side as we wandered beneath the arching green trees, flowers blooming at our feet on either side of the trail. It was almost like walking through a painting now.

"Nothing big. Just a small fine dining place. A few signature dishes. Just a few tables."

"Hmm," Tess said, and I wondered what she was thinking. I glanced down at her, glad to see a look of calm contentment on her smooth pretty face. My blood warmed at the perfection of her profile, my nerves jangling as I thought about what it would be like to touch her, to kiss her.

"Hey," I said, stopping our progress.

She turned, a question in her eyes, and I realized I had nothing specific in mind to say.

"I just … thanks for coming out here with me today," I tried. My voice was lower than it had been a moment ago, almost a whisper.

She stared up at me, her dark lashes lush against her pale skin, her plump pink lips slightly apart as she considered me.

"Yeah," she said. Her lips parted like she was going to say something else, but no words came out. Instead, she stepped a tiny bit nearer, and every nerve in my body went to full attention.

"The park is really …" I trailed off, my mind going blank as she pulled her bottom lip between her teeth and then let it go. My skin was buzzing and my dick was suddenly straining inside my jeans, no doubt thinking about those perfect lips the same way I was.

Hell, I wanted her, but I couldn't make a move here. She'd already made it clear I shouldn't muddy the waters by touching her, and I wasn't a guy who was going to touch a woman who'd asked him specifically not to. But when she reached between us and took my hand lightly in hers, I swear a fuse in my brain burned right out. She was touching me and that simple touch felt better than any sex I'd ever had in my life. There was something here. Something incredible. I hoped she could feel it.

"Hey," I breathed, unable to manage much more with the incredible buzz in my mind at the contact of her skin between my fingers. I was slipping into caveman mode, instinct taking over. Did cavemen say, "hey"? Maybe surfer cavemen.

I let my fingers graze gently up her wrist, stepping nearer until we were just inches from one another, each of our chests rising and falling with shallow breaths. Anticipation hung in the air between us, along with a rich fecund scent that reminded me of sweat, sex, and earth. God, I wanted to drop to the ground right here and bury myself in Tess. I wanted to feel that supple body in my hands, beneath me, on top of me, around me. But I needed to move slowly. Let her set the pace.

She was staring up at me, a fierce look in her eyes, a burning dare that I knew I'd take.

I bent my head forward and she closed the distance between us, grazing her lips against mine and then lifting her eyes again. I kissed her softly, mimicking her shy touch, her hesitation. When I pulled back, her eyes were shut, her cheeks glowing with high spots of color, and those petal pink lips were slightly open as she breathed. She was perfect. She was everything.

She tilted her head up more, inviting me back, and I didn't hesitate this time, dropping my lips to hers again as my arms slid around her perfect body. I devoured her then. I should have been gentle, tentative. I should have waited for her to take the lead, to tell me this was all right, that this was what she wanted. But I didn't wait. I didn't ask, and her answer came in her actions, not in her words. I teased those lips open with my tongue and crushed her body against me, felt her panting breaths as she came alive beneath my lips, my hands. Every part of me was straining to get closer to her, and when she ground her hips into the aching swell in my pants I nearly lost it.

After a few moments—a few hours?—I broke it off, pausing to pull myself back together.

My head was spinning with desire, my hands possessively sunk into her body, caging her to me. I released her, running a hand through my hair, suddenly nervous as Tess just stood there, regarding me as she gasped for breath, making those glorious breasts beg for my attention.

And then she attacked me.

CHAPTER TWELVE
TESS

Chalk it up to a long-unplanned celibacy, or life with Gran. Call it overexposure to sunscreen and bug spray. We can call it whatever we want, but the plain simple truth was that I had a movie star kissing me like he'd never get enough of me and I wasn't about to push him away just because it made no damned sense at all. I'd figure that out later. But for now, desire was ricocheting around inside my body and Ryan McDonnell was pressed up against me—all hard and firm and muscled—and I never wanted it to end.

Maybe this was nothing but pretend to Juliet, but it felt a hell of a lot like heaven to me.

Ryan's hands were all over me, massaging my back, gripping my ass, fisting my hair. He trailed kisses over my jaw, nibbling at my neck and making me gasp and wrap myself around him, trying to get closer and needing friction, needing something I couldn't even define.

I pressed myself hard into him, feeling his erection at my center and gasping without meaning to—it was heady knowing I'd caused that. And 'that' was impressive, I was pretty certain.

Unless he had a flashlight in his pants, and I didn't think he did.

After a few moments, I stepped back, trying to catch my breath.

Ryan did the same, rubbing a hand through his now very mussed hair, a slow sexy smile spreading over his lips. My heart leapt into my mouth as I looked at him, my brain attempting to process that I'd just been kissing Ryan McDonnell. Who was not, I reminded myself, Juliet's boyfriend.

It was a lot to wrap my head around.

"That was better than a Sasquatch sighting," he said, as I moved back to his side and took his hand, heading for the lighthouse out on the beach.

"Really?" I asked, feeling a little shy suddenly, even though my heart was bobbing around excitedly inside me. I kissed Ryan McDonnell. I was holding his hand. Was this actually my life?

"Way better." He bumped my shoulder lightly as we walked. "I'd still like to see him though."

The packed dirt trail beneath our feet turned to sand as we walked, holding hands, meandering.

The wide swath of beach that curved around the southern tip of Maryland's peninsula jutted into the water where the Potomac met the Chesapeake. Ryan plopped down in the sand, grinning up at me as he took off his shoes and then nodded for me to do the same as he stood back up. I did, rolling my jeans up to my knees, and then we stepped together into the cool water lapping at the edge of the beach.

"Look at that," he said, looking out to the east. "It just goes on forever, doesn't it?"

I bit my lip, unsure whether he needed correcting. Today didn't seem to be about teaching Ryan Maryland's geography, but I couldn't help it. "Well, it goes until it hits the eastern shore, so I guess it depends on your definition of forever." I lifted a hand to turn his chin to point southward instead of east. "There, look that way. That pretty much goes on forever."

"Geography was not my strong suit in school."

"What was?" I wanted to know more about him. I knew what the magazines wrote, I knew him as the hero I'd seen in the theaters, but I didn't know much about the real guy besides what he'd told me today.

He took my hand and threaded his fingers through mine, the warmth of his palm soaking into my skin and contrasting with the coolness of the water swirling around my ankles. "School was not my strong suit in school," he said. There was a low sadness in his voice that made me look up into his face. Given what little he'd told me about his childhood and his father's work, I had the sense he might have had other things to worry about besides homework and classes.

"Switching schools a lot is hard, I bet," I offered. I was speaking from experience. I'd had to switch after my parents died.

I couldn't see his eyes because we were both wearing sunglasses against the glare of the sun reflecting off the water all around us, but I could guess at the sad acceptance they might hold. He nodded and then moved closer to me, his body pulling me like a magnet. His arms slid around my waist, and he pulled me into him, one hand coming up to cradle the back of my neck and the other staying low, holding me near. "How is it that you fit me so perfectly?" he asked, in a low whisper that made it seem like a rhetorical question.

My mind had been working on a similar question as my hands slid up the firm broad planes of his back, my breasts tightening as they pressed against his hard chest. My head nestled beneath his chin, and in the circle of his arms I had a strange sensation of shelter, of a safety I really hadn't sought, but was comforted to find. "I don't know," I answered.

We stood there for several minutes, our bodies pressed

together, the sweet sting of salt on our lips, and then Ryan dipped his head and kissed me again. This kiss was slow and sweet, his lips soft and his tongue teasing, not demanding. Where he had taken before, back on the trail, now he asked permission, sought acquiescence. And I gave it willingly, molding my body to his, opening my lips to his seeking tongue.

It sounds cliché, but the kiss really did make me dizzy. Maybe it was the angle of my head, or the way my body felt like it didn't fully belong to me now that his arms were supporting it, but the world alternately slowed and sped up, the bay roaring in my ears and the sand slipping beneath my toes as water washed it from under us. When Ryan released me, my heart hammered and my breathing felt erratic. I stared at him next to me for a long minute, unsure what was happening here, totally confused about how to proceed. What did one do when one was suddenly forging a completely unexpected romantic interlude with one's movie-star crush? This was uncharted territory, at least for this Manchester sister. Sightseeing did not seem to be an appropriate focus at this point. "Want to get a drink?"

He nodded, but angled his head toward the lighthouse, a two-story building with a light tower on the top. "We don't get to see the lighthouse first?"

"You can't go inside unless you're on a tour," I told him. "Plus, it's haunted."

He dropped his chin and grinned at me. "Maryland is rife with supernatural beings, isn't it? Sasquatch, ghosts, and a woman who I'm pretty sure is a figment of my imagination."

I shook my head. "What?"

"You can't be real."

We turned to walk back toward where we'd left our shoes. "Why not?" I asked. "Why can't I be real?"

"Because I've been dreaming about you my whole life."

I didn't know what to say to that, but my chest warmed. I

pretended to focus on putting my sandals back on my feet, pretended my stomach wasn't turning flips and my mind wasn't spinning at Ryan's words.

As we got back into the car, I stilled just as I was about to throw it into drive.

"Do we need to worry?" I asked him. "What if you're seen with the wrong Manchester sister in public?"

He frowned, but shook his head lightly. "I honestly don't get recognized often, but I guess it's a concern. Do you know any place kind of off the beaten path? Maybe not too busy?"

I did.

We drove for a while then, up the peninsula and out a long road to a quiet café with its own dock. It was a local's joint, not one tourists ever found, and they made great margaritas.

"Are you looking forward to the party?" Ryan asked me once we were settled.

I nodded, though a little ball of anxiety rolled around in my gut as I sipped the drink that had just been delivered. "I am, but Gran is a little tough to please, really. I don't think she wanted to have this big party."

"So it's for you?"

"It's for posterity," I said. When he lifted an eyebrow in question, I went on. "She's turning ninety. And she's kind of a fixture down here. Granny used to be really involved with the local community. She was a teacher and a principal and then a district administrator. Did you know that Granny used to be the President of the National Education Association?"

He shook his head. "That's impressive."

"But now … she's not senile, not at all. It's hard to pinpoint exactly …" I trailed off, thinking how to explain the eccentricities that I'd grown accustomed to. "But she's just a complete individual at this point, and she doesn't enjoy following society's rules anymore. So I never know how she'll behave around people."

He made a small "hmm" that sounded like agreement or understanding.

"She might even refuse to come out once the party starts. She's so wrapped up in Warcraft." I already knew I would recruit Juliet's huge bodyguards to go in and pick up her gaming chair and carry her out to the tent if that happened. One way or another, she was going to attend her party.

This made Ryan chuckle. "I've played that game. I see how it becomes addictive." He took a fry from the basket the waitress delivered and ate it slowly. My eyes were drawn to the full lips as they moved, the motion of the strong jaw. My stomach flipped again. I liked him. I wanted him. But he was only here another couple days. Was I already in too deep?

"Actually, my dad is kind of like that," Ryan said, snapping me back to reality. "He's inappropriate around people now. But mostly, I think he's angry."

"I thought you ran away?"

"I did, but after things got easier for me, we connected again. He lives with me now. I moved him in a couple years ago, when he got lost driving one night. The police took him home and called me when they took away his license."

"Is your dad sick?" I didn't really know how to broach the topic of dementia. It wasn't something people enjoyed talking about.

His mouth made a tight line and he looked down at his hands. "He's mostly angry, I think. He hates relying on me, on anyone. But he's gotten really frail and confused, and he can't be totally on his own."

I watched Ryan talk. Something soft moved through his eyes when he talked about his dad, and the angles of his face lessened, softened. He had a tender heart, I realized. He loved his dad, even though he'd run away from him. My own preconceived notions about this man loosened a bit.

"Do you and your dad get along now? Even though you left?"

"Things are never quite that easy, are they?"

I thought about that. My own childhood had been. At least up until Mom and Dad had died and Juliet had become … Juliet. "I guess not." I sipped my drink, and when he didn't say anything else, his gaze drawn to the birds dipping and crying over the dancing river, I let myself pry a bit. "Why'd you leave?"

He blew out a breath, tilting his head as his gaze met mine again. "I honestly didn't think he'd notice. I was invisible at home. He was so busy with work. Mom had already left, so I knew I was invisible to her."

I knew what it felt like to be invisible—but I'd never felt that way at home. Not with my parents and not with Gran. I couldn't imagine not having at least one person on your side. "But he did notice when you left, didn't he?"

"He looked for me. Says he did, anyway. When I got my first big role, he got hold of my agent on the phone."

"Wow." I imagined running away, making myself famous with no support at all. I guess in a way, that was what Juliet had done. I wondered if she felt invisible at home as Ryan had. I'd always figured she was just too big to live in a small town.

"And so… what happened then?"

"We had a few lunches. Eventually I took him to a movie premiere. When he couldn't drive or live alone, he moved in with me. But I think he's going to need more care soon."

"Like a home?" I thought about Gran, about her fear of having to leave her house. Luckily, her health was good, but I knew it could change. Poor Ryan.

"Yeah. There's a place that's really nice. But it's expensive."

I might've gaped a bit. "But you're a movie star."

He laughed. "I guess so. But the place I'd like to be able to set up for dad is movie-star expensive."

"That's part of why you agreed to this thing with Juliet? The money?"

"Definitely. That's most of it."

"What's the rest?"

Ryan dropped my eyes then, stared into his drink. "I guess part of me still wants to do well enough to feel seen. Does that make any sense? To feel good enough at something. Successful."

I didn't know what to say to that, so I just nodded, sipping my drink. How could a movie star feel invisible? I understood why I felt that way—I lived in Juliet's shadow. But Ryan McDonnell was a legitimate movie star—people definitely saw him.

"I think maybe sometimes we don't see ourselves very clearly," I said, and it occurred to me I could have been talking about each of us.

He tilted his head, one side of his mouth lifting as he considered my words. And then he lifted his drink.

"To being in a completely new world," he said. "With an amazing woman, who I see very clearly." He raised his glass. I tapped my own to it and smiled. And as Ryan and I sat in the sun out over the water, drinking and laughing together like old friends—or new lovers—I realized that he wasn't a movie star.

He wasn't the guy who had inhabited my fantasies (and those of lots of other women in America). He was just a guy. A guy who loved his dad, who wasn't sure where he was going. A guy who for now, anyway—was sitting here, having a drink with me and laughing in the sun.

I let myself relax and enjoy the attention, and that was probably when I accidentally fell a little bit in love with Ryan McDonnell.

CHAPTER THIRTEEN
RYAN

Water lapped around the pilings of the pier and the sun beat down on the wooden planks at our feet as I sat with Tess in a corner of a patio that felt more and more like a different world. Or maybe it was just that this was Tess's world —and it was so far from what I'd grown accustomed to that it felt like I was on a different planet.

Though I was not Juliet famous anywhere, in Hollywood I was interesting enough to have to pay attention. Here, I was just a guy. And I was starting to really like it.

There were no photographers lurking around, no one waiting outside the front doors of the restaurant when we finally walked out and strolled down the boardwalk late that afternoon. There was no one staking out the car where I leaned Tess back and devoured her mouth and neck again before we actually got in. There were no flashes, no shouts, no jarring realization that I was visible to everyone in the world and somehow still even more invisible now that I was famous. They saw me—kind of, but it was like the real me faded away a little bit more with every single camera click, every flash. I had none of that to worry about here. There was just this beautiful day. This beautiful girl. And me. And for the first time in such a long time—I felt like someone really saw me.

"You're quiet," Tess said, as she navigated the car back toward Gran's old plantation house.

I was stunned by the beauty of a place I'd never even thought about, a place I hadn't known existed. And by the peace I felt here with Tess. "I'm just enjoying everything," I told her, letting my hand rest on her knee as she guided us confidently home.

"Must be nice to get a break from the pressure of Hollywood," she said. Her voice told me she knew what those pressures were—and why wouldn't she? Her sister was one of the most celebrated actresses of our generation. "Or are you eager to get back? Now that your career is poised to take off?"

"It's tempting to think about running away again," I said honestly. "I had kind of forgotten places like this exist." I didn't want to go back to Hollywood—knowing this weekend would come to a close and my life would return to normal, or my version of normal at least, wasn't a welcome thought.

"Backwoods towns where nothing ever happens, you mean?"

"Gorgeous untouched places full of amazing people," I corrected, looking at her.

A smile flitted over her lips, but then they pressed into a straight firm line before she spoke again. "But your life is on the other coast, and you'll go back in a day or so."

Hearing her voice the reality made me wish desperately I could change it. "Right," I said slowly.

Tess sighed and I watched her drive for a moment, a little vein in her neck pulsing and her forehead wrinkling and then smoothing as thoughts appeared to pass beneath it. I squeezed her knee, wishing I could see inside her mind, see what was causing her to look tense all of a sudden. She inhaled sharply at the contact and then pulled the car over to the shoulder and stopped, turning to face me.

"Look," she said, her voice at once soft and steely. "I know this is probably a fun diversion for you, going to a place you've never heard of and wowing the locals. Watching the country girls swoon—that kind of thing."

Shock formed a bright ball in the front of my mind. Is this what Tess thought? That this time with her was some diversion? I was shaking my head slowly. That was so completely not what this was.

"But this is my real life here, and I'm having a hard time figuring out where to place this. For you it's a weekend trip. For me ..." she trailed off and I wondered desperately what she'd been thinking. What she wouldn't say.

"Hey," I said, pulling her aviator shades from her face. "This isn't just a distraction," I told her. "I didn't know I'd meet you. I didn't plan this at all." What else could I tell her, what could I say to make her see that she felt like so much more than a fling to me? "I didn't expect any of this."

"Any of what, exactly?"

"You," I told her. "The attraction I feel for you. The ... the feelings I'm having for you."

"You just met me."

I nodded. She was right, but the fact it was crazy didn't make it less true. "And so you're saying you don't feel it too? You don't feel anything for me?"

She watched me, and I saw a flicker of fear or uncertainty dance across her face for a brief moment. "I'm not sure it matters."

I took her hands, made her face me fully. If she felt any bit of what I felt for her, I had to make her see that we had to explore it, give ourselves a chance. I felt like I was standing on the edge of something incredible—a once-in-a-lifetime opportunity. And if I didn't take it, I'd always regret it. "Yes, it does matter."

She shook her head. "I'm just trying to be realistic, Ryan. I'm trying to protect myself. You're a freakin' movie star. Girls fall in love with you all the time, and if I become one of them, my heart will break when you leave, when you go back to California, pretending to be dating my sister ..."

"Maybe we won't do that now." I said the words, knowing I had an ironclad contract. I doubted I could get out of it. And I didn't want to hurt Juliet, as much as I wanted to be free to pursue Tess.

"What? Pretend?"

"Go back." I don't know what made me say it. I wanted to stay here. At least for a while. Maybe it was time for a break, for a vacation. For something new. Maybe my career was slipping because I had nothing to fuel it, nothing in my real life to lend to the characters I played. But still, I shouldn't make promises I couldn't keep.

She laughed, a sound that was sharp and disbelieving. "Right."

"What if I stayed a little while?" I asked her. "What if I just stayed?" I threw this out there, knowing it was all but impossible. I had Juliet and Dad to think about. I had a movie to film —the one that was going to launch my career to the next level. What was I saying?

Tess sighed and pulled her hands from mine. "That's the beauty of being a movie star, I guess. You can just pretend things for a while. You get paid to do it."

My back straightened as the jab of her statement hit home. "What does that mean?"

"People don't just decide to move like that, Ryan. And what about your career? And your dad?"

I did need to worry about Dad. They were holding a place at the retirement community for him, but I needed to come up with the down payment, and it was more than I'd put on my own home. "I hired a nurse to stay this weekend. I can ask her to stay longer." But it wasn't a solution. Not really.

Tess was looking at me, a strange expression on her face. Finally, something that looked like resignation replaced the skepticism I'd seen there. "You're crazy," she whispered. "People don't do that." She pulled the car back out onto the road and didn't say anything else.

I didn't know what to say, either. I'd already said a lot of things I'd never intended to. Crazy things. Who did that? Who met a girl one day, kissed her the next and then told her he was thinking of moving across the country for her just to see what it would be like? Crazy people. Surfer cavemen people, maybe.

"We can just pretend none of this happened if you want," she said as we pulled back into the long drive in front of her house. "Just a fun day to remember. Nothing else."

I hated that idea and it caused a visceral reaction, my stomach turning my muscles tensing. I frowned, wishing I could see her eyes behind the shades. "Is that what you want?"

She laughed, but it held no joy at all. "What I want? I just want to go back to my regular life where I know what's going on and movie stars don't pop in, kiss me, and then make wild proposals about moving to Maryland."

"What if we went back to before I made a wild proposal, and just stayed at the kissing part?" A man could hope. Maybe if we took things more slowly, Tess would come around. I knew—because I'd been the one kissing her—that there was more here than she was willing to admit. If I could give her some time, I suspected she might be more willing to admit it.

She parked and turned off the engine, turning to look at me and finally pulling the shades from her eyes. "My sister might be good at pretending," she said. "But I live in the real world. I like you, Ryan. I mean—I was kind of helpless in all this. I've been kind of in love with some image of you forever, so how could I not want to kiss the real thing?"

A thrill went through me at the thought of Tess being in love with any version of me. I was about to speak, my mouth eager to fill the void, to apologize some more for being rash, to convince her that I could back off. But she lifted a finger and I snapped my mouth shut.

"We could maybe go back to the kissing part," she said. "But you can't say things about moving, about staying. It's too much, way too soon, and even though I know you're insane and it would never really happen, I wouldn't be able to keep myself from believing just a tiny bit that you might do it. And then, when you left …"

"I get it." Her explanation was perfect, and it rekindled the hopeful desire that had been growing inside me. Her eyes were sad as she spoke, those full lips nearly pouting as she said the words, and I just wanted to pull her into my arms again. God help me, I wanted to bury myself in her and never come up for air.

"Okay, good." She turned and got out of the car, and I realized my heart was racing. I took a deep breath and stepped out too, catching her hand before she could climb the steps to the house.

She turned and looked up at me, her eyes cloudy and dark. I traced my thumb over her full bottom lip, and she exhaled, her warm breath dancing over my skin. I leaned in slightly, careful and slow, not sure exactly where we stood now. But Tess didn't back away, and as my lips brushed hers, all hesitation slid away. Whatever else we lacked—geographical convenience, similar lifestyles—we made up for in chemistry.

Our lips met and Tess's tongue found mine, pieces of a puzzle that had been apart too long. She nipped at my bottom lip, pulling a groan from somewhere deep inside me, and then somehow she was in my arms, and our bodies reached for one another. My mind was flying, my body warming and tightening, and I wondered if her intention was to have her way with me here in the driveway, because she was suddenly so driven. Her hands were pulling at my clothes and the most incredible little moans were coming from her mouth. I wanted to throw her down and take her right there on the ground.

As images of Tess in every compromising position I could imagine flew through my mind and my body began to take over, a sound came from the front porch, causing us both to freeze.

We turned our heads to find Granny standing just outside the front door, grinning, wearing a T-shirt with a picture of some kind of warlock or something that said "Max DPS" above it. The fire inside me was doused. Caught.

And Gran still thought I was dating Juliet.

"Oh God," Tess moaned, stepping away from me. "Gran," she said, as she stood up.

"Hello, kiddies," Gran said, her voice full of glee. "Mr. McDonnell, you sure do get around. Tess, I thought this was Juliet's boyfriend." She turned the grin on me.

Shit, shit, shit. I was already failing both Manchester sisters. This would make things very difficult between Tess and Juliet, not to mention with Gran. And between Juliet and me. I looked at Tess, not sure how much to say.

"It's kind of complicated, Gran," she said. "I'm sorry we're so late. Ready for dinner?"

Gran didn't seem interested in moving inside quite yet. "Young man, I thought I warned you earlier ... You don't get to mess around with both my granddaughters."

"No ma'am," I said, "I would definitely never do that." I was suddenly terrified of this tiny fierce woman, and could only imaging how scary she must have been as a school principal.

"Tell me this then. Since you're Juliet's boyfriend, am I

wrong in assuming it was you I heard Juliet with in her room last night, then?" she asked, narrowing her eyes at me. "All that husky moaning?"

Tess turned her head and gave me a look to match Gran's. Dark, angry, suspicious.

I had no idea what the old woman was talking about, but a frenzied worry began to build in me. "No," I said, hoping my confusion made me sound innocent. "Definitely not me."

"Hmm." Gran didn't say anything else as she turned and went back inside the house, but Tess was watching me warily. I hadn't slept with Juliet. Not last night, not ever. I thought back to the moans I'd heard myself coming from her room—I'd thought maybe she was sleeping, but they had possessed a slightly sexual tone, now that I was thinking about it. What was going on?

"I swear," I said, turning to Tess. "I told you the truth. If Juliet's got someone in her room …" I'd just gotten Tess to a place where she was willing to explore this thing between us. If she believed I was playing her, she'd never trust me. My heart pounded and felt like it might actually explode.

"Ryan," she said, her voice low. "You're the only guy here."

"We're sleeping in separate rooms," I said.

"Doesn't sound like Gran is talking about sleeping," Tess said.

"You know," I said, scrambling to follow Tess up the steps. "There is the security team."

She turned then and shot me a disbelieving look. "Juliet is not getting together with a bodyguard." Her voice dismissed the possibility of continuing the conversation, and I swallowed the rest of my protest. Whoever had been in Juliet's room, it wasn't me. I just needed to make sure Tess believed me.

CHAPTER FOURTEEN

TESS

As I made dinner, I spent the evening trying to understand what was happening. With me, with Ryan.

With Juliet. She kept disappearing and reappearing, looking confused and distraught and honestly nothing like herself. Dinner was a strange affair, and after the day I'd had with Ryan I just wanted to go to bed and think about things. Tomorrow was Gran's party and the press would be back, and so would half of Southern Maryland. I needed to be ready.

"I'll get these," Ryan said, clearing plates from in front of us.

"So polite," Juliet said, smiling up at him.

I stared at the look that passed between them, trying to see whether there was something there, whether they were keeping something from me. But why would they lie about being together if they really were getting together? It made no sense. I swung my gaze to Gran, who was sitting smugly at the head of the table, rolling a joint like that was something all ninety-year-old women did at the dinner table.

"Gran, at the table?" I sighed.

She shrugged and winked at me. "Big raid in an hour."

That game was going to be the death of me.

"Get it out of your system tonight. Tomorrow you have to dress up and be the center of attention and act like a proper old lady."

She sighed deeply. "I had kind of hoped I'd keel over before then. I guess there's still tonight ... sometimes wishes come true, right? You got to kiss your Hollywood crush, after all."

It was like the room had just caved in on my head. I cringed and my blood turned to sludge as I swung my head to look at Juliet. What would she think? She'd just told me this afternoon that she and Ryan were pretending. What if she thought I'd been kissing him when I believed they were together and I just didn't care?

"Jules," I whispered, about to explain.

Ryan had just walked back into the dining room in time to hear this proclamation and he looked at me, wide-eyed.

Juliet's head snapped to me. "You kissed Ryan?" She looked angry.

Shit. This was all getting too complicated. "What? No," I lied, not sure why I was lying now. "I mean ... no, he's your boyfriend, right?" After all, we were still playing that game for Gran, weren't we? I nodded my head toward Gran in an exaggerated kind of don't-forget-Gran-doesn't-know motion.

Of course Gran knew more than any of us ever gave her credit for, but as far as Juliet knew, the ruse was still going on.

"I mean, he was in your room last night," I went on babbling, feeling a little out of control. One of the security team in the hallway stepped around the other door and stood behind Juliet, listening more intently than I thought he should have been. "Moaning huskily, right Gran?"

"I wasn't eavesdropping," Gran said quickly. Too quickly. Then she flushed and looked ashamed of herself, slumping slightly. "I couldn't help it," she said. "You were so loud. I haven't heard those noises in this house since I quit watching Erika Lust films." She shot a defiant look at Juliet and then rose. "I'm expected elsewhere." She picked up her joint and walked slowly from the room past the guard who had slipped back around the corner.

"What the hell is going on?" Juliet asked, looking between Ryan and me. "Are you two hooking up?"

"No," I said.

"Yes," Ryan said.

Oh God. Why couldn't he just go be gorgeous and perfect in Hollywood and let me pine away for him when I watched his movies? Why was this happening in real life? I stared at my sister, whose mouth had dropped open slightly as she turned to look at Ryan. "Seriously?" Her voice was an accusation.

Ryan stood at the end of the table where Gran had been. His mouth opened and then closed, and then I watched as something seemed to solidify in his eyes, his expression steeling. "Jules," he said. "I didn't plan it. It's just ... I think there's something here." He gestured toward me.

It was the same thing he'd been saying in the car, and while I knew it was crazy, a warm certainty bubbled up inside me before my very rational thoughts forced it back down. This was not a thing. It couldn't be anything.

"Yeah, something's here," Juliet said. "My little sister's here. And she doesn't need you barreling into her life and screwing everything up, just to leave when your next movie role takes you to Timbuktu."

"What are the odds there'll be another movie in Timbuktu?" Ryan said. "I think it was just that one—"

"No," Juliet said, standing up. "You don't get to charm your way out of this one, you ... you ..." Juliet seemed to be searching for a scathing word to blast him with as her hands balled into fists and her lips formed a tight line. In the end I found myself wishing she'd reached out for help in the creative slur department because she finished up with: "Man!" She hissed the word at him, but it fell a little flat. I sensed that Juliet was unleashing her own anger at men in general at Ryan on my behalf, and I realized we still hadn't really talked. I had no idea what was actually going on with my sister, but it couldn't be good.

"Not much of a burn," I muttered, shaking my head. This entire thing was ridiculous. "Listen, guys," I said, wanting to run away, to stick my head beneath the comforting pillow of my normal life. I forced myself not to look at Ryan, keeping my eyes on Juliet. "Let's just pretend none of this happened," I suggested. "If you're hooking up, that's perfect. That's what you want everyone to think anyway, right? And you'll be gone in a couple days, and Gran and I can go back to our regular lives. Whatever happened between me and Ryan, which was pretty much nothing, was just a lighthearted fling. It was nothing." I glanced at him, the pain and disappointment on his face more pronounced than I would have expected. A little ache developed in my chest and I pressed a hand against it.

"Um …" Ryan said, looking confused.

"No. Look," Juliet said, stepping in close to him, her face reddening. "You're here because I'm doing you a favor. I didn't bring you here to charm the pants off my naïve little sister and break her heart. That's not what this is about. This is about—"

Naïve little sister. Right. That did it.

I stood up too, my blood heating. "You." I finished her sentence for her. "Everything is about you. It always has been. Right, Jules? And this, this weekend—which was supposed to be about Gran, by the way—has become a media circus so you can show the world that Juliet Manchester is just fine after her nasty divorce. And what makes a woman fine? Another man, of course! So you picked one off the man tree to help you out, and we all have to play along, right?"

Juliet and Ryan were both staring at me now, but I'd

opened the door to the closet full of secret feelings and they were all rushing out into the light. My mouth marched forward and it was almost like I was standing apart from myself, watching in horror as I told my sister everything I'd ever felt. In front of Ryan.

"It's so hard for you to imagine that maybe someone might actually be interested in me, isn't it? It's just completely outside your realm of experience. After all, what do I have to offer? I'm the short one, the fat one, the unpopular one ... I'm Juliet Manchester's little sister, right? That's all I've ever been, and with you around, it's all I'll ever be."

Ryan had moved to stand closer to me now, looking torn. I wanted to throw myself into his arms and let him comfort me, but another piece of me just wanted to throw things, flip tables and scream at him for bringing me to a place where all these feelings demanded to be unleashed.

"No, Tess ..." Juliet said, but I had twenty-five years of repressing my real feelings and I couldn't stuff them back in now. I realized I was burning down my world, destroying whatever relationship I had with my big sister, but I couldn't go on pretending I was happy to stand in her shadow. I wasn't. I deserved to be seen too.

"Let's just get through tomorrow night's charade and then you can all go back where you belong," I said, turning. "You can take your fame and your angst and your enormous security guards and just go home. Both of you." I walked out of the dining room past one of the looming guards and headed for the stairs; glad to hear no one was following me. Chessy shrieked as I walked by, and I felt a strange chicken-girl kinship. Like she got me somehow.

In my room, I paced, waiting for the confusing mass of feelings inside me to stop swirling around long enough to sort through them. But they didn't. Age-old anger and hurt at being perpetually in Juliet's shadow had risen within me, making me feel vulnerable and young. And whatever had been bubbling between Ryan and me wasn't helping. I wanted him. God, did I want him ... and the weird thing was, I was pretty sure he was legitimately interested in me, too. Or else he was a better actor than I thought.

The way we'd sat this afternoon over the water, holding hands on the tabletop talking like we'd known each other for years ... why would he fake any of that? And the kissing. My God ... the kissing. Just thinking about the way his arms felt around me, the way his breath had been hot on my neck, in my ear ... it had muscles deep inside me tightening in expectation.

Shit.

He had to go back home. They both needed to go. I just had to survive watching them pretend to be a couple for the press at the party tomorrow, and then I could go back to my regular life, teaching people to kayak, leading tours, watching over Gran ... being alone.

Shit.

"Tess?" Ryan's voice came through the door, interrupting me mid-angst. Everything in my body heated, knowing he was just outside my bedroom door, but my mind took charge.

"I think you better just go away," I told him, squeezing my eyes shut in an effort to steady my voice.

The door opened.

"God, you don't listen, do you?" I said, my body vibrating the second he was in the room with me.

He shut the door behind him and stepped forward, his bright eyes on mine, those perfect full lips slightly parted. He pushed a hand through his amazing messy hair and sighed.

"Tess, I know I'm doing everything wrong," he said. "But I can't leave here until I know what's between us." His eyes searched mine and I took a step toward him without meaning to. "I know there's something here," he went on. "I can feel it, and I know you feel it, too. And look, I mean ... I don't know what it is. Because I've never felt anything like it before. All I know is that I want you like I've never wanted anyone, anything, in my life. I want to be near you, to breathe you in, to hear you talk and see you move, and ... God, I sound like an idiot."

My mind stopped pounding around inside my head looking for an answer and the room stilled at his words. I believed him. And all I wanted was to believe him long enough to never have to think about all of the complications surrounding us again. I took another step toward him and suddenly I was in his arms, our mouths locked together in a desperate kiss that sent spirals of longing through my limbs, my stomach, my mind. I closed my eyes and light burst in flashes inside my mind as I let go.

A little voice deep inside was screaming at me to be stronger; not to be that girl, not to be the girl every woman probably became near Ryan McDonnell. But I couldn't stop now, and I let Ryan's hard firm body press against mine and pull me into him because the temptation was too great and I was weak. Maybe my sister was right and I was just her naïve little sister.

Maybe I didn't care.

Maybe I could use people too, and maybe I could use Ryan tonight. Maybe it didn't mean anything.

I stopped thinking.

I Just. Let. Go.

His mouth was hot and insistent on mine, and his hands were sliding over my body, gripping and rubbing, pulling at my clothes. I slid my palms up beneath his T-shirt, up the firm solid muscle of his back, feeling the corded strength on each side of his spine. And then the shirt was gone, and I was unfastening his pants, pushing them down his body as he undressed me. We stumbled around the room, pulling off items of clothing and sliding our hands over each other, and it felt like neither of us would ever get enough of the other's hands or mouth.

I heard myself whimpering, a needy wanting sound I didn't even know I could make. But I needed more. I needed so much more than hands and tongue and … Oh, God. Ryan lifted me and spread me out on my bed, my legs still draped over the side as he knelt between my legs and demonstrated an entirely different kind of talent apart from acting. "Oh my God," I moaned, as my hands fisted the bedspread.

Ryan's tongue and fingers worked together to drive every last rational thought from my mind until I was nothing more than wanting and need, and then he was over me, claiming my mouth again, pressing every inch of his hard firm body into mine. His hands and mouth were on my breasts, his tongue and teeth turning me into a woman I didn't recognize as I writhed and thrashed beneath him. My hands were in his hair, grabbing at his back, reaching for his perfect ass.

And then he was gone and back, ripping a condom packet in his teeth and gazing down at me as he knelt over me. "Is this okay?" he asked, holding himself in one hand.

I'd never been a particular fan of the male anatomy. Which isn't to say I didn't appreciate it in a utilitarian sort of way. The truth was, I'd only had occasion to really look at a few examples up close. But Ryan's cock was smooth and thick, and … beautiful.

I stared at it for way too long, probably grinning like an idiot. I took him in my hand then, nodding, since the power of speech had left me again. I slid my hand along his length and watched his eyes drop shut. His enjoyment made me feel bolder, and I took his balls in my other hand as I stroked him, watching as his body shuddered. I took the condom from his fingers and rolled it down his length, his eyes fixed on my hands.

"Yes," I finally managed to say.

And nothing else was needed, because then he was there, pressing into me, gently at first and then thrusting, my hips matching every motion until I thought I'd split into a thousand pieces. I wrapped my legs around him, raked his back with my nails and held on, knowing I was seconds from falling apart. And with me holding him so tightly, the movement changed and shifted, became deeper, slower. Ryan was rubbing something deep inside me, some spot that felt like fire and wanting and need, and with every movement I became more desperate for release.

And when it came, it wasn't an explosion. It wasn't sudden, or shocking or a surprise. It was exactly as I'd known it would be, considering my ultimate movie-star crush was in my bed, in my arms, inside me.

It was consuming and overwhelming, like a wave building inside me and rolling over us from the inside out. It went on and on, a pulsing, living, moving thing that bound me to him, that separated me from everything else I knew. That made us whole together. And when it ended, I was left helpless and happy, whole and yet changed, in the arms of a man with whom I was very afraid I might be completely in love.

CHAPTER FIFTEEN

RYAN

Sex with Tess was exactly what I thought it would be.
   Perfect.

Everything about this girl was exactly perfect for me, and if I said that didn't scare the hell out of me, I'd be lying.

And now I held her in my arms, our hearts beating against one another as our breathing slowed, and I didn't ever want to let her go. I had to make her see what I already knew.

"Ryan," she breathed. "Let go. You're suffocating me."

"Oh God, sorry." I rolled to the side and relaxed my grip, but I wasn't letting go. I'd already decided. I couldn't let this girl go.

Tess smiled up at me, her eyes cloudy and half-closed. But even as I smiled back down at her, her features cleared and the edges of her perfect little mouth began to turn down. "Ryan," she said, beginning what I knew was going to be some kind of apology or excuse, something I didn't want to hear, didn't want her to say.

I dropped my mouth to hers and stole the words with a kiss. Tess moaned again into my mouth and I wished I could keep her there, connected to me forever.

But her hands dropped from my back and moved to my chest, pressing me gently away, cold fear replacing the certainty I'd been feeling. "Ryan," she said again, breaking the kiss and moving so that I slipped out of her, a sensation that threatened to break my heart in a way that surprised me completely.

"Tess, don't," I said. "Don't tell me all the reasons why this is wrong, or why it can't work. Don't pretend it didn't happen, or that you didn't feel everything I just did. There's something here. And if I have to do all that again to prove it to you, I'm willing."

That earned me a tiny smile, but then she shook her head, the dark waves spilling over the pillow in a soft blanket. "I love the idea," she said slowly. "But the reality is what we need to look at."

I hated reality. I wanted to stay as far from reality as possible right now. "I don't like where you're headed with this." I moved in to kiss her again, to see if maybe one more perfect kiss could move her to the mindset that was so clearly rooted in my own brain.

Tess rolled off the bed and reached down, pulling her shirt up to cover herself as she stood. "Ryan, this was nice." She blushed then, and my heart stuttered at how incredibly sexy she looked standing there, blushing and looking down at the floor as she tried to cover her perfect full breasts with her T-shirt. "I mean, honestly, I just had sex with Ryan McDonnell. Forget that no one would ever believe me if I told them, or that this was pretty much my ultimate sexual fantasy fulfilled."

My brain detached for a moment, letting itself turn over the words she'd just said as my ego soared. But the words she said next pulled it back.

"But you're leaving the day after tomorrow, and I'll never see you again unless I go to the theater. And you'll be pretending to be with Jules, and you'll both be back to your version of regular while I'm here in the real world ..." she trailed off, and looked around as if she was seeing her room for the first time. Then her voice softened, cracking and nearly breaking my heart. "And … look … Could you maybe just go? This is too much. It's too hard."

I sat up, shaking my head. "It doesn't have to be, Tess."

She wouldn't look at me, wouldn't meet my eye. She picked up my clothes and handed them to me, then stepped back quickly, and I shivered. Could this really be over?

I disposed of the condom in the little trashcan next to her desk and got dressed, watching Tess the whole time as she tried not to look at me. How could I fix this? I wasn't sure I even knew exactly what was broken.

"I want to stay," I told her.

"Just go," she said, and her voice was so full of remorse and sorrow that I felt my heart wither and shred as I did what she asked and watched the door click shut behind me.

I walked slowly down the hall in the quiet house, pausing when I heard Granny yell, "Gotcha, sucker!" from somewhere down below. Juliet's door was shut, and I knew I should probably just go to sleep, but I didn't want to be alone.

I hadn't come to Maryland looking for anything specific, but maybe if I was honest with myself I could admit that I'd been searching for a while. For something. And when I'd found Tess here, in this quiet life surrounded by beauty and water and simplicity and the constant lingering smell of pot, there was a big part of me that was trying to drop anchor. Because all of this felt right.

Well, maybe not the pot part.

For lots of years—even before Hollywood swept me up and gave me direction—I'd moved from place to place, been a stranger. When you only stay places for a year or two at a time, you start to realize there's no point in trying to find people to care about, or to care about you. You're just going to leave them anyway. My parents had actually taught me that lesson early on.

And after I'd gotten my break, when I'd been in Los Angeles for a few years, and had some friends, I began to understand that friendship meant something different when you had money, when your name meant more than what was inside of you. If anything, I was more alone now than I'd ever been before, despite more people knowing me than I'd ever dreamed was possible.

But Tess was different ... she made me feel like I was part of something else, like maybe together, we were something bigger. Tess gave me a glimpse of a different kind of life, one where you stayed in one place because that was where you belonged, because that was where your heart lived and where you were loved. Because it was where you were supposed to be.

I stood in the center of the hallway in that old house for a long moment, listening to the house creak and groan as the wind wrapped around it outside. My mind turned and twisted, working to make sense of how unexpectedly this place had infiltrated my mind, my heart—how completely Tess Manchester had taken over everything uncertain and afraid in me and lit a path that made more sense than anything in my life ever had. I stared at the gentle glow of light cast up the stairs from below. It probably wasn't the right move, but I followed that light and Granny's gleeful shouts down the stairs and into a small office in the back of the house.

The old lady was wearing a headset, sitting in front of a huge monitor in the biggest swiveling chair I'd ever seen. The screen in front of her showed a huge colorful world and a group of cartoony characters gathered around carrying a wide range of weapons and wearing bright armor and robes. I recognized it immediately.

I'd told Tess I knew the game because of my college roommate, but that had only been because I was embarrassed to admit I played it myself.

"Playing a paladin?" I asked, stepping into the darkened room, which had a lingering cloud of pot smoke hovering in the air.

Granny's head whipped around, her small eyes alight. "Level sixty-eight," she said. "You play?" Her wrinkled face pulled into a grin as she stared at me. I cringed a bit—this lady probably didn't have a very high opinion of me, and I wasn't sure what she thought now.

I stepped into the room, pulling a chair up next to her. "I have played. The last movie I did was on location, so I haven't in a long time."

"Ah," she said, turning back to the group on the screen.

"I always liked to tank, too." The tank was the warrior in a group, the guy who drew the bad guys from everyone else, who took the brunt of the attack. It was the character I always played—in the game, on the screen.

"Paladin?"

"Death Knight," I told her, which earned me another grin.

"So there's some substance behind that pretty face," she said, swinging her chair around to face me. She was regarding me with a thoughtful expression, and I had the sensation of being evaluated—like Granny could see past the surface now that she was looking at me so intently. It was both uncomfortable and strangely enjoyable. As she stared at me, the group of other players on the screen moved away, leaving her standing alone.

"I didn't mean to interrupt," I said, gesturing at the screen. "I think your group is heading out."

"Nah," she said, a little cackle at the end of the sound. "I got in a group with a bunch of twelve-year olds. That's the problem with playing on the east coast. I have to stay up pretty late to play with grownups, since bedtime for those

California juvenile delinquents doesn't seem to be until midnight."

I laughed, knowing exactly what she meant. "I remember what that was like—kids getting in crazy fights about drops and disagreeing about everything." I might have played a little more in college than I'd admitted to Tess.

"It's like babysitting sometimes," she said, pulling the headset from her head. "But I bet you didn't come in here to talk about Warcraft." She gave me the sharp-eyed look again.

I tried a smile. "I just heard you awake, and thought I'd say hello."

She narrowed those watery eyes at me and made a clucking sound. "I think you need some guidance." She smiled. "Too bad the only person around is an old pothead."

I let out a laugh. She was charming and funny. It was a welcome relief. "I need something," I agreed. "I just don't know what it is. And I have a feeling I might know where Juliet got the acting gene. I think you want people to believe you're just an old pothead. I think it's your cover."

She squinted at me as she took in these words. Quietly, she said, "It's easier to see what's really going on if everyone thinks you're an idiot."

It wasn't a whole lot different than being treated like the 'talent' and talked around in contract meetings. "I get that, actually." I sighed, leaning back in the chair next to her. "So do you see what's really going on here? With me?"

"You need to decide," she said. "You can't have both my granddaughters."

I shook my head. "Yeah, I know." Then I realized she still believed I'd come here as Juliet's boyfriend and that Juliet had asked me not to tell her the truth. But I couldn't have Tess's grandmother believing I was that kind of guy. "No, I mean … it's kind of complicated."

"Only because you're a man," she said, her voice taking on

a sage old lady tone. "Your dick complicates everything where beautiful women are concerned."

"I'm not arguing with that," I chuckled, enjoying her straight-shooting nature. "But there's more to it …" I looked at her for a long minute, and I knew my assumption about her cover was on target. Where I'd first believed Tess's granny was a crazy old pot-smoking lady, potentially senile, now I saw a sharp woman who had enough experience to live exactly the way she wanted to and made no excuses for it. There wasn't a senile bone in her body, I realized. "I'm not really with Jules," I told her. "That was a pretense for the press."

The clucking noise again, and Granny shook her head slowly. "The world you live in," she said, trailing off.

"I know. It's a mess." I sighed, and found my mouth opening again, words forcing their way out before I'd had a chance to think about it. Gran's attention, and the atmosphere around her that just seemed to suggest she knew and understood things she didn't always share, had me babbling. I told her about my childhood, my current career, and even my dad.

"He's been diagnosed with dementia. I have to take care of him, but I travel a lot for work, and I need to move him somewhere they can look after him. But it has to be a home—not just a place, does that make sense?"

Gran's lined face was solemn. "I do understand that. I've had friends in the same situation. What does your dad think?"

"He's scared. He knows he isn't always tracking lately." My chest hurt when I talked about what was happening to my dad.

"Of course he's scared. And so are you." Gran's bright eyes held mine. "There are very nice communities, though."

"Yes," I agreed, trying to sound optimistic about the place Dad and I had chosen in Los Angeles. "The good ones are really expensive."

"No problem for a movie star, though?" Her voice suggested she might know it was going to be a leap.

"This star hasn't been much of a star for a while," I said, feeling the pressure this situation was causing, the need to push my name back up the list of viable leading men. "But I'll figure it out."

"There's a very nice place here, too," Gran said, glancing at her screen. "I visit one of my good friends there. I'd imagine such places are less expensive here than in a place like Los Angeles, but what do I know?"

"I'm starting to think you know a lot," I told her.

She tilted her head then, her eyes widening as her hands folded on her lap, little wrinkled fingers working together. "You have a lot on your plate. And what about my granddaughter, Tess?"

I dropped her gaze, staring down at my own hands. "I'd really like to be with Tess." I risked a look back up at the old lined face. She was smiling.

"But …?"

"But I think my life is too complicated for her."

"Un-complicate it."

If only it was that simple. "I want to. I want it more than anything … but she … I don't know. Maybe she doesn't believe me."

"Seeing is believing, Ryan. Show her you're serious."

"I tried, I mean, I want to try."

"Do or do not. There is no try."

"Yoda? Seriously?" I laughed.

"People say we look alike," she said, pursing her lips and lowering her chin in a little pose.

"No they don't," I said, grinning and relieved to feel lighter suddenly, less burdened.

"Maybe not, but Yoda was wise," she told me. "And he knew how to deliver the sagey oracle shit with panache." She turned her chair back to face the computer screen, where her character stood still, waiting for her to return.

I watched as she pulled the headset back on and leaned forward, her hand on the mouse and the other on the keyboard. Her Paladin ran forward, and for a while I just sat, watching the young strong version of Granny on the screen moving over endless green hilltops in a fantasy world where she could go wherever she pleased, do whatever she wanted. But watching made me feel tired—Warcraft was one quest after another. Each achievement was just a key to unlocking harder challenges. There was really no rest, no end.

In some ways, wasn't that what my life was like now? Roaming endlessly, moving from one thing to another?

I wanted solidity and permanence. I wanted more.

I said goodnight to Granny and went up to my room, set up my laptop and opened a browser. An idea had been brewing in my mind, and the more I thought about Granny, about Warcraft, the more exhausted I felt. I wanted something else. Something real.

CHAPTER SIXTEEN
TESS

Sleep was like an old trusted friend who was on some exotic vacation texting you selfies with tropical umbrella drinks and hot dive instructors just when you needed her most.

Bitch.

After Ryan left the room, I lay awake and took stock. My body hummed with memories of his touch, and my muscles were soft and languid, the result of the very best orgasm I'd ever had. And while my body purred as I lay in my bed alone, my brain whizzed and jerked, trying to find some way that all of this would be okay.

But it wouldn't.

Because I was an idiot. I'd let myself become completely absorbed in the dream of Ryan McDonnell. In the few days I'd actually known him, I'd gotten much too close, and I knew when he left I was going to be broken. I'd entertained a fantasy, let it wind itself around my heart, and now it was going to be very hard to release.

How could the boring standstill world of my everyday life ever compare to the dream of having a movie star sweep me off my feet?

But that was what this was. Just a dream. Even if Ryan was not really with Juliet, there was no chance he was going to be with me. I knew myself too well for that.

I was Tess Manchester, largely invisible to men.

On the plus side, that gave me a lot of time to pursue activities, and had allowed me to build a successful business and construct my life pretty much the way I wanted it.

The down side was ... well, it was pretty obvious as I looked around my room. My life often felt empty.

When the sky outside began to lighten in infinitesimal amounts, I slipped out of bed, feeling as if I hadn't slept at all. I couldn't remember every single one of the dark minutes that had ticked by, but it felt like I'd been awake to mark each one's slow passage. And I stood beside my bed now with a weight in my chest and fog in my mind. And more than one hundred guests coming tonight for Granny's party, not to mention the press for Juliet's article.

Perfect.

I slogged downstairs in my pajamas, looking for coffee, and nearly had a heart attack when I bumped into Juliet in the living room.

"Oh, Tess!" she said, looking every bit as surprised to see me at o'dark-thirty as I felt to see her.

"Hi," I said. I wondered why she was wandering around the house this early in her pajamas, but then realized I was doing the same thing. Maybe she couldn't sleep either. "Getting coffee," I told her, my best effort at conversation still making me sound like fuzzy and dense at this hour.

"Good, yes," she said, following me to the kitchen. Her quick answer and the glance behind her made me think my sister was hiding something. For a split second, my suspicion rose again and I peered around in the darkness for Ryan—could they really be together as Gran had insinuated? Was she sneaking around down here with him? But that didn't make a lot of sense, and it was far too early for me to worry much about it.

While the coffee brewed, we sat across from each other at the small round table in the kitchen, each of us lost in our own thoughts. Once the pot was done, and we each had a mug between our hands, Juliet looked up at me. "You doing okay?"

Shame crept over me, a wet rag that smothered other feelings and pushed my shoulders down into a slump. "Jules, I'm sorry about what I said last night." I said the words, mostly because I loved my sister and wanted to mend things between us, less because I was actually sorry.

"No, you were right." She sipped her coffee, put the mug back down and traced the rim with her finger. "I know it isn't easy being my sister, Tess. I know I make it hard."

"It's not always you … it's just all the things that come with you now," I said, wishing things could go back to how they were when we were kids. Just sisters. Just life.

"Things like Ryan?"

I sighed. I had no idea how to sort through the feelings I had for Ryan.

"He's a good guy, Tess. And we're not together, so …"

"So now it's okay with you?" I raised an eyebrow at her over my mug. It had been very not okay last night.

She shrugged. "You were right. It's not about me, and it's not up to me. I want you to be happy, and lord knows you need to meet someone. Your life has revolved around salt water and Granny and other peoples' adventures for way too long. You're verging on spinsterhood."

"I'm twenty-five."

"Well."

I shook my head. Facts had never gotten in the way of a good story for Juliet.

We were both silent for a while, drinking our coffee as the sun lifted to the horizon and spread rays of pink and orange across the sky, every color reflected in the surface of the water at the edge of the lawn. Juliet watched me, and finally put her mug down.

"You should give him a chance," she said.

Even if geography wasn't a problem, we were worlds apart. How could a man like Ryan ever really be happy with a simple woman like me? He might be charmed by Maryland now, be having fun entertaining the fantasy of leaving his glamorous life, but he'd never really do that. And I'd be a fool to think he could.

"It would never work out." How could it? We lived on opposite coasts and our lives couldn't be more opposite. "There's no way I'd ever move to California," I said. "And last I checked, they aren't making any big movies out here. We don't even get to see half the movies down here—I had to drive up to DC to see that one you did that won Sundance."

"Well, they don't always distribute the smaller films as widely ..." Juliet began, but then she shook her head. "This isn't about film distribution. If Ryan wanted to make it work, he could. And so could you."

I didn't have an answer for that. I might be willing to put in the effort, but Ryan had too much going for him in California. Why would he go to the trouble?

"Just don't close the door on it," Juliet said. "I want to see you happy."

"Because it's about you?" My feelings were still raw, sensitive. My words might have come out a little sharp.

Sadness filled her eyes then, and she dropped her head low, staring into her mug. "It's not," she said. "I'm sorry if I've ever made you feel that way."

I felt immediately guilty. I was confused and hurt, and I was taking it out on her. "I'm sorry too," I said. "It's not your fault, Jules. What did Mom used to say? The only person who could make you feel something was you?"

She tilted her head and shot me a half-grin then. "But I bet Ryan could make you feel something if you gave him a chance." She waggled her eyebrows suggestively.

God, she was right about that. He made me feel all kinds of things, and just thinking about it set off little signal fires in my bloodstream. "Who says I haven't let him already?" My body still warmed when I thought about his touch, and something inside my chest had changed, too. He'd gotten inside me in more ways than I wanted to admit.

Juliet gasped. "Good girl," she laughed. "More of that!"

I shook my head. If only things were that simple. "Not today. Today's Granny's party. And your friends from the magazine will be back. Today Ryan's *your* boyfriend, remember?"

She actually looked upset for a second before recovering herself. "Right." She shook her head and pushed her hands into her hair on either side, "I'm sorry," she said. "I'm sorry I brought my mess out here and made it your mess."

"It's okay, Jules," I said, and I meant it. My sister really had been through a lot lately, and I vowed to remember that today as I watched her pretend to love the man I thought I might actually be falling for. "It's okay." I stood and walked around the table to kiss the top of her head before heading back upstairs. It was going to be a long day, and I needed to get ready.

CHAPTER SEVENTEEN
RYAN

When I got downstairs, Tess was nowhere in sight. Juliet stood near the kitchen sink, and I stepped up beside her, hoping not to startle her.

"Hey," I said, my voice soft. I wasn't sure where I stood with Juliet at this point—I kind of felt like my time with Tess had invalidated our agreement, but then again, that was the entire reason I was here in the first place. And the contract did not have any clauses I remembered about hot younger sisters.

Juliet jumped at the sound of my voice, her hands jolting upward and sloshing coffee into the air and down the front of her shirt. "Oh!"

"Sorry," I said, reaching for a paper towel and handing it to her. "I didn't mean to scare you."

She shook her head. "No, it's not your fault. I was … I was just a million miles away."

"Everything okay?"

"Yeah," she said, the trademark smile failing to light her green eyes. "Yeah, it's fine."

I didn't quite believe her, but she didn't seem eager to share, so I let it go. "What time is the crew getting here today?"

"Not sure," she said, sounding as unenthusiastic as I felt. "Sometime this afternoon, I think."

"So if I were to disappear for a few hours, that would be okay?" I asked.

"With Tess?" Juliet asked, and I was surprised at the little jolt of pleasure I got at just having her name mentioned around me. Plus, hearing the suggestion so easily from Juliet that Tess and I might be spending time together was a nice change from being yelled at over the dining room table.

"No," I said, maybe too quickly. "I have a couple things I need to take care of."

"In Maryland?" Her tone was skeptical.

"Um," my brain spun, looking for some kind of appropriate cover. "Just need to get out for a bit," I said finally. "Look around. See some of the country."

"Sure," she said, a half smile making it clear she didn't think I was going out to sightsee. It didn't really matter, though. Juliet didn't need to know my plans. I wasn't even sure about my plans. "Just be back by two or three, okay? I think the crew is due by five for sure."

"Definitely." I hoped I'd be able to get things handled by then. I slurped down some coffee, grabbed a muffin from the basket on the counter, and headed for the front porch, watching a car pull up just as I stepped out.

I'd set this all up the night before, so I went down the wide front steps and right up to the dark hulking car, popping the passenger side door open.

"Hey," I said, greeting the woman at the wheel. She was pretty in an overdone kind of way. Big sunglasses, dark hair slicked into a knot on the back of her head. She smiled at me, and then something in her face shifted as she realized she might know who I was. I hadn't given her the name I usually went by, so when I climbed into the passenger seat of her big SUV, I allowed her a few minutes to recover from the recognition and surprise I saw on her face.

"Are you …?"

"I am."

"And you want to buy a house in Maryland?"

"Maybe," I said, smiling. I'd come up with this idea as Tess had talked about the drastic differences between our worlds. I didn't want to live in a different world from Tess. And maybe if I could find a little piece of home for myself in this world… well, maybe things could work.

"But …" she trailed off, her mind finally clicking into place as she shook her head lightly. "I'm sorry, I just. .. I'm just surprised, that's all. I'm not used to showing houses to movie stars."

I didn't bother to tell her that Juliet Manchester was just a few feet away from where we sat, drinking coffee distractedly inside in front of a window. Tess had said most of the folks who'd lived here a while knew Juliet was from this area, that most knew exactly which house had been hers.

I gave the realtor my trademark grin. "It's fine, but I am on a bit of a schedule today. Can we look at those waterfront houses we emailed about?"

"So you were serious about the … the big ones?" She pulled the car out of the driveway and back down the long lane as she eyed me sideways.

"I was." I was as serious as I'd been about anything since running away. I might not have a plan for after I bought the house, but I knew that I wanted a piece of this world, this serenity and beauty. I was pretty sure I wanted it even if Tess wasn't in it.

"It's just," she waved a hand. "People sometimes want to see them. You know, look but not really because they want to buy." She blushed and giggled then. "I'm not saying that's what you're doing."

"That's not what I'm doing," I confirmed.

"Okay," she said slowly. "Well, okay then." She seemed to finally settle into the situation. "Well, it's a pleasure to meet you, Mr. McDonnell, and I sure hope we can find something you'll like today."

"I hope so too, Jessica." I settled back into the leather seat and watched the lush green trees fly by the sides of the car as we sped down one country lane after another. Thankfully, Jessica didn't seem big on small talk once we'd settled the confusion over my identity, and she was happy enough to just take us to the first property on our list.

"This is seven-thousand square feet," she said, opening the grand front doors into an expansive foyer that spread out into a wide open living room with high ceilings and exposed wood beams. From the floor-to-ceiling windows on the back side of the house, I could see the water sparkling just beyond a sloping green yard. A long wooden dock stretched out into the glassy dark water.

"Six bedrooms, six baths," Jessica continued. "A chef's kitchen, a first-floor master and mother-in-law suite in the basement downstairs. The rest of the bedrooms are upstairs."

We wandered the house and the property, and then looked at four more that might have been built by the exact same builder for the exact same homeowner. The sun was high in the sky and I knew I'd need to get back to Juliet and the magazine folks soon as we left the last ridiculously big house. I wasn't finding what I'd imagined. I'd fallen in love with Tess's house—the history, the girl too. I knew I wouldn't find a house with Tess Manchester waiting for me inside, but I didn't want a cookie cutter builder home I could have gotten anywhere.

"These are all beautiful," I said. "At the risk of being one of the people you were talking about ... I don't think I'm in the market for anything so ..."

"Over the top?"

"Right. Maybe something a little different? A little less… new?" I watched Jessica scan through some more listings on her iPad before she turned to me.

"There is another I'll show you if you have time. It's less ostentatious. More unassuming."

"Still on the water?" I didn't know why that was so important to me, but maybe growing up poor had made me feel like you'd really made it in life when you could wake up every morning and see an endless expanse of water stretching out in front of you—something most people would never be able to afford in California, even movie stars. And there was plenty of water here in Maryland.

"Yes, still waterfront," she confirmed. "More land than the others, actually. Just not as much house."

"Let's go!"

I ARRIVED BACK at Tess and Juliet's house later than I'd planned, and was disheartened to see several long black town cars and a van already pulled into the circular drive in front of the house. The magazine folks were already here. Would they already be interviewing Juliet, wondering where her new boyfriend had gone off to? Had I forced her into another bad situation?

"Here he is," Juliet called, opening the front door just as I thanked Jessica and pushed closed the passenger door to her car. I heard her sharp intake of breath through the open window as she spotted Juliet, but she was gracious enough to pull away rather than linger.

"I'm so sorry I'm a little late," I said, adopting my boyfriend persona even as my stomach turned at the falseness of it all.

"It's fine, hon," Juliet said, reaching a hand toward me.

"Did you find what you needed?" She turned her movie-star smile on me and I forced a smile back.

"Yep, found exactly what I was looking for," I told her, wishing I didn't have to pretend for the rest of the day, that I could just fast forward to the future, to everything I'd dreamed of when I'd walked through the little waterfront cottage with the sweeping back deck nestled beneath two-hundred year old oaks on the edge of the Patuxent River.

I wanted to find Tess and tell her that as soon as I'd seen the place, I'd seen us in it, seen us standing in front of that railing looking out at the water, seen us laughing in the expansive kitchen with toddlers running at our feet, seen us nestled in bed in the grand master bedroom, which also faced the water. I'd seen the future I wanted; now I just needed to show it to Tess. And make her believe in it.

I knew it was crazy. I knew it was all too fast.

But I didn't care. Because I knew Tess was the only woman for me, and I just had to prove it to her.

As soon as I was done pretending to be in love with her sister.

"Hello, Ryan." Alison Sands greeted me, and I took a deep breath, telling myself this was the end of the pretense. That soon, I'd be able to be exactly who I really was. That soon, I could tell Tess I was staying—or at least making a second home here; ask her to give me a chance.

"We'll just do some more casual shots now that we've got the afternoon sun," Alison said, waving a hand at the golden light draping the back lawn. "And then you lovebirds can go change for the party."

"Perfect," I said, wrapping my arm around Juliet's waist and pulling her near. "That sounds perfect."

This was going to be the hardest role I'd ever played.

CHAPTER EIGHTEEN
TESS

I watched from the top of the stairs as Ryan wrapped his arm around my sister's waist, looking like the happiest guy in the whole world. He'd been gone the entire day, so there'd been no opportunity to talk about what had happened between us, to get myself straight. Clearly, he wasn't worrying about it or obsessing over what could or couldn't be between us.

Of course he wasn't. He was a movie star—a spectacularly handsome Hollywood playboy, and a good actor. It was practically his job to make me feel like I was different, like I wasn't just another girl on a long list of girls. And he was too good at his job. I had felt special. I had felt unique. But in the cool distant shadow of his absence, I found my rationality and logic. And there was no way Ryan McDonnell had an ounce of real interest in a water adventure instructor from the middle-of-nowhere, Maryland. It just didn't make any sense.

I'd spent the day alternately overwhelmed by ridiculous anticipation of what might happen between us, buoyed by a ridiculous hope, and berating myself for being so easily infatuated, so easily convinced there was something there. I'd been the one to push him out of my bedroom, so it didn't make much sense that my heart was still squeezing at the thought of him, pushing me to hope for impossible things. My mind was the rational voice, the one I needed to listen to. It had been only two days, after all. And he was a friggin' movie star. I was Tess Manchester. This was clearly not my life.

Now, as I stood watching Ryan's strong firm body pressed up against the side of my sister's lean petite form, all my doubts crystallized and hardened into facts.

It had been fun. It was a fling. It didn't matter what he said —weren't actors known to be flighty and unreliable? Actually he was the only actor I knew besides Juliet, so I really had no solid evidence, but it was easier to trust my own assumptions than to put any faith in something as impossible as Ryan McDonnell being interested in me.

I continued down the stairs and slipped through the hall to where Gran sat on the back porch, reading on her ereader.

"Hey there," I said.

"Manhattan?" Gran lifted a silver shaker my way and nodded her head toward her own half-full glass.

"It's a little early," I said. "Gran, you need to be somewhat sober tonight. All these people are coming to see you."

"Is that a yes?" She picked up a second glass and poured, handing me the brownish liquid with a smile that would have looked right on the face of a seven-year old sneaking candy. Gran's spirit helped bring my mood up—it always had. Life wasn't perfect for her, but she never failed to find the things in it that she could laugh about. I needed to practice that.

"Those magazine folks here to capture more of your sister's silliness on film?"

I sipped the drink and pressed my lips together instead of spluttering. "Strong," I managed, once I'd swallowed what felt like fire down my throat.

Gran sighed and put her ereader down. "Tess, I want you to be happy, you know that, right?"

I wasn't sure where this was coming from. "Thanks, Gran. I want me to be happy too. And I am, mostly."

"Mostly." She cackled, her eyes clouding as she gazed out at the rolling lawn. "Hoping your life is mostly happy. There's a greeting card sentiment for you."

Just then Jack and Chessy strolled by, Chessy trotting contentedly at Jack's side. They seemed to have come to some kind of understanding. I thought maybe Chessy was actually happier than I was at this point.

"I hope he's not thinking of taking my attack chicken when he goes back to LA," Gran said.

I was about to respond when a familiar—if not altogether welcome—voice came around the side of the back porch. "Hey, Tess, hey Gran."

"Tony," Gran said, her lack of enthusiasm for Tony Myers made more evident by the amount of rye she'd already had today.

"Hope it's okay, me popping in early," he said, pulling up a chair. "Thought maybe you could use a little help getting things set up."

Something in me warmed at Tony's nearness. He was like a sibling—one I'd always been able to trust, to rely on. But there had never been anything else between us, and I felt regret too, that I couldn't be happy with the man right in front of me. I smiled at Tony, who'd been part of my life since Kindergarten. We'd been boyfriend and girlfriend once for about six minutes in seventh grade, and I didn't think Tony had really ever gotten over the breakup. (Which involved me telling him that I wasn't as much a fan of Angel as I was of Spike, and that our fundamental *Buffy* disagreement probably meant we weren't a good match.)

He was a good-looking guy, really. He'd grown into his lanky build and had filled out, and his light brown eyes were so familiar I couldn't help but feel a little bit at home every time I found my gaze on his.

Tony was a nice guy, he was practically family. And he had loved me and looked out for me my whole life. He was the one guy I'd ever known who didn't prefer my sister to me, who didn't wish I was her. He was the guy who'd come when my parents had died while we were in school, who'd been here every time I'd needed a friend.

And he'd only tried to kiss me seventeen or eighteen times since seventh grade. Tony had never given up on me.

As I heard Ryan's voice roll from inside the house, laughter at something my beautiful sister had said filtering through the afternoon air to where I sat, I realized that maybe I needed to give Tony a real chance. Tony was safe, he was reliable and certain. Tony was the man I was most likely destined to be with—the fact he was a constant in my life seemed like a message from the universe. Trying to change it was like trying to change fate.

And that was pointless. No matter how much my insides jumped when I thought of Ryan. Or how completely still they were at thoughts of Tony.

"That's so nice of you," I told Tony, smiling at him and coaxing my heart to warm. "You're always so thoughtful."

Gran was squinting at me, her mouth twisting on one side in clear confusion. "Tess, really? That's how you're going to play this?"

"I don't know what you're talking about," I said, picking up my drink and finishing it in one long burning swallow. Unfortunately, the Luxardo cherry at the bottom followed the liquid directly into my windpipe.

I tried to cough politely, to coax the cherry from my throat, but it wasn't working and I couldn't get enough air to pop the thing out. I tried to swallow, but that wasn't working either. My lungs began to constrict, panic starting to fizz at the edges of my mind as I realized that I was choking. People died from this. Every day.

A wheezing gasp came from my mouth as I pointed at my throat and swung my gaze desperately between Tony and Gran.

Fear swelled in me as my vision began to waver and I motioned to my throat, a horrible sucking noise coming from my mouth.

Tony's eyes widened at me in horror as I mimed the Heimlich maneuver.

He shook his head lightly, looking from me to Gran and back again. Tony was not going to save me. I was doomed.

"Oh for fuck's sake," Gran said, rising and coming behind me. "Tony, you putz, I'm not strong enough, come here."

Terror was spiking through me. I was going to die. Choking on a cherry.

At least I'd gotten to sleep with Ryan McDonnell first.

My vision was starting to black out when I felt Tony's arms come around me, Gran's voice distant but still sharp, telling him what to do. He squeezed me hard, once and then again. And the cherry popped out of its spot and flew onto the porch, landing with a plop.

I sank into a chair, sucking breath and then immediately launching into a coughing fit as Tony let go and guided me by my arm. My mind raced with the near-death experience, flying through all the things I'd been taking for granted. Air. Water. The taste of Wensleydale cheese.

"Holy cow, Tess. You scared me." Tony was sweating and gasping as if he'd been the one choking.

"Jesus," Gran muttered. "Now I need another drink for sure. Tess, Let me die first, will ya?"

I was coughing and gasping, happy to feel the air finally coming back into my lungs.

"Thank you," I wheezed at them.

Tony grinned, looking pleased with himself, and took the chair next to me as Gran sank down and dropped her head into her hands.

"Fuck," she mumbled, lifting her head to finish off her own drink.

"Sorry, Gran," I said.

"I'm glad I was here," Tony said, clearly congratulating himself.

"Me too," I told him.

"Why?" Gran shrieked. "If it had been just the two of you, you'd be dead on the porch by now. Haven't you ever taken a first aid class, you redneck?"

Tony's jaw dropped open and I frowned at Gran.

"He just saved my life, Gran."

"Bullshit," she said, shaking her head. "I saved your life." She stood up, picking up her shaker and empty glass. "Don't get old," she said. "No one gives you credit for anything once you're old." She shuffled inside, shaking her head.

"Thank you," I said to Tony, meeting his eyes and immediately wishing I hadn't. There was so much longing and adoration there, it felt like a heavy coat someone had tossed over me that I couldn't get off. It was smothering. And now that he'd saved my life? I'd probably never get rid of him. I realized I could never be the girl he wanted me to be and he'd never be the guy I wanted.

We sat for a little while as I regained my breath and let the adrenaline fade. Finally, I stood, thinking maybe I should try to give Tony a real chance. The guy had just saved my life. I shouldn't make rash decisions in the aftermath of almost dying. Maybe if we spent more time together feelings would kindle.

"Tony, I probably do need some help, out here in the tent."

I led Tony across the lawn and into the tent, where centerpieces needed to be arranged and placed, and place cards needed to be put in their correct locations according to the table map I'd spent hours making. I tried not to think about the last time I'd been in the tent, about the way Ryan had nearly kissed me in the doorway. Trying, however, was not doing. And my skin prickled and warmth rushed between my legs as I thought about the night I'd spent in Ryan's arms.

Tony. I shook off my illicit thoughts. I needed to focus on Tony.

"Thanks for the help," I said as we worked. "I really appreciate it."

Tony grinned over the tables at me, his eyes shining. "Tess, you know I'd do anything for you."

I did know that. And I willed my stomach to flip when he smiled at me, willed my blood to heat like it did when Ryan came near. But it wouldn't. Of course it wouldn't. Tony was just Tony. No matter how rational I wanted to be, my libido seemed ridiculously won over by the fact that Ryan was a movie star.

That's all it was.

And of course I'd known Tony far too long to have those crazy feelings for him. It was unfair to expect them.

"Do you need a date for the party tonight?" Tony asked as we finished up inside the tent. "I'm going to head back home to get dressed, but I'd love to be your plus one if you're up for it."

I smiled at my old friend, torn between telling him the truth and potentially leading him on just to save his feelings in the moment. "That'd be great, Tony. I'll see you in an hour." It would be easier to see Ryan and my sister together if I had a fake date too.

He leaned down then and kissed my cheek, a sweet gesture I hadn't expected. I smiled up at him as he stood back up, the smile I'd known since childhood on his handsome face. "See you soon," he said, squeezing my hand and then turning to stride long-legged across the rolling green of our back lawn. My stomach churned at the hope in his face.

"You're screwing it all up, Tess," my grandmother called from the porch, where she sat with her second Manhattan of the afternoon.

Shit. Gran was going to be drunk, and I was screwing it all up.

Beside her, Ryan and Juliet stood, the camera crew just ahead of them and the reporter waving her arms and directing them to sit with Gran. Juliet's eyes were on the reporter, her movie star smile glowing at full wattage.

But Ryan's eyes were on me, and I felt my blood rushing inside my veins under his hot gaze.

CHAPTER NINETEEN
RYAN

I watched from the back porch as some tall guy emerged from the party tent out on the lawn with Tess, kissing her on the cheek and holding her hand before he left, sending a yearning gaze her way as he crossed the lawn back to wherever the hell he came from.

When Tess turned and saw me watching her, her eyes snapped quickly away, and she went back inside the tent, leaving me with a swirling ball of energy building inside my chest, making me unsure about anything. I didn't even know what this feeling was exactly, but there were undeniable elements of jealousy and anger. And confusion—had I so totally misread the situation? When she'd pushed me away the night before, had it been for some reason I wasn't aware of? Something more than I'd thought?

Because I'd thought she was just a little scared. Maybe a little worried about trusting something that was happening so fast. Maybe a tiny bit unwilling to believe I could be falling for her.

But I was. I had. Maybe at first sight.

"Ryan," Juliet whispered, her breath a tickle under my ear.

"I really need you to focus. If you screw this up now ..." she trailed off and I pulled back, finding her eyes.

"What's wrong?"

Juliet angled her head toward where Alison was chatting with the photographer about the shot we were supposed to be taking.

"Sorry," I whispered.

The photographer spent what felt like lifetimes getting the shot just right. I suspected part of the issue was that Gran was refusing to smile when they asked her to.

"Get some shots of what ninety really looks like," she cackled.

"Gran," Juliet hissed.

"I'm not some complacent old toddy," Gran complained. "Can't I look a little bit badass? It's my birthday."

Once the photos were done and Alison had taken the photographers out to the tent to see if they wanted to capture any photos in there before the party, Juliet leaned in to whisper again.

"My lawyers called while you were out. Zac is saying I cheated first, and he's found three different men who swear we were together during my marriage."

I didn't know Juliet well, but I had no doubt she'd been faithful in her marriage. You could just tell she wouldn't cheat. Plus, no one who cheated repeatedly on their husband would be as upset as she'd been the past week over the marriage ending.

"If they find out this is all a farce, it'll just make me look like a liar. People won't know what to believe."

My heart iced over inside my chest. If we called it quits after the weekend or let things just fade, the media would certainly speculate about the reasons. "So we have to go on pretending."

She nodded.

"For how long, Juliet?"

A tear escaped the corner of her eye and I reached up to wipe it away without even thinking about it. "I don't know."

The future I'd seen before me, shining and bright with possibility after this weekend suddenly dimmed into uncertainty. Tess knew I didn't love her sister, but maintaining an ongoing pretense would mean going back to Los Angeles, keeping up appearances and photo opps. It would mean being away from Tess. It would mean honoring my contract with Juliet, securing my own future and my dad's. But it would also mean giving up the potential I'd only begun to discover here.

"Over here, you two!" Alison called across the lawn.

Juliet took a deep breath and my hand, and I followed her down the porch steps, wishing for once in my life I could be in control of my future.

"Just a few more sweet kisses?" Alison suggested, and I considered maybe shoving her little notepad down her throat. Instead, I pulled Juliet Manchester into my arms and kissed her as convincingly as I could manage. She pressed herself into me, met my lips with hers, opened her mouth to my tongue. The moves were right—but everything about it was wrong.

"Oooh, that was a hot one," Alison cooed as we broke apart. And that's when I saw Tess, standing in the door of the tent watching us. Her eyes met mine for a brief second, and then they squeezed shut for a beat too long, and she turned and disappeared inside the tent.

"Shit," I heard myself mutter. My muscles tensed and it took everything I had not to sprint across the lawn to her.

"Are all men complete morons?" Gran asked loudly from her table at the porch. She held up her ereader as if she was just asking a rhetorical question to the book she was reading, but I had a feeling the sharp old eyes didn't miss much. And her mind missed even less.

She was right. I was a moron. But I was contractually obligated to be one.

Eventually, the camera crew dispersed for the afternoon and we were released to go get ready for Gran's party. By that time, Tess had disappeared and even Gran had left her spot on the back porch. Caterers were bustling about the kitchen and event staff populated the lawn and tent, moving in audio equipment and setting up odds and ends. For what it was worth, the party looked like it was going to be amazing.

"I'll come get you when I'm ready," Juliet said as we parted ways at the top of the stairs.

"Okay," I agreed, uncertain whether I'd survive the party.

"Hey," she said, pausing outside her door.

I looked over my shoulder at her.

"Thanks for all this. I know it's a mess."

"It's okay," I said, but I didn't believe it was anymore. It wasn't okay to lie to the world and forsake my own heart and Tess's. It wasn't okay to give up a chance at real happiness—the first one I'd ever found—all in the name of a lie.

The weekend had been touted as a career opportunity by my agent. It had been a job, basically. And now it felt like I was being shoved down a path that I knew led to a sheer drop off or into a deep unswimmable lake. It led somewhere I knew I didn't want to go, and I couldn't seem to turn around.

When Juliet's door shut, I turned and walked down the hall toward Tess's room. Maybe if we could just talk for a few minutes, maybe if I could tell her everything now, in the quiet privacy of her room, then I could assure myself that I wasn't insane, and tell her the kiss she saw had been more acting. More pretense.

I'd tell her my plans, see the gleam in her light eyes and know I'd made the right choice—for both of us. And I'd have whatever reassurance my silly heart needed that the guy on the lawn had been no one to her. A friend. Or … someone. I couldn't imagine who he could be to Tess. All I knew was that he was someone who felt it was in his right to kiss her. To hold her hand.

Someone I didn't like very much but found myself envying a lot.

I needed to talk to her.

But as I stepped near to her door I heard Gran's voice from inside. "I told you, no frills, no lace!"

Evidently Tess was helping Gran get ready for the party.

Now wasn't a time to talk. My stomach fell.

I turned and went back to my room, pulling my tux from the closet and heading for the shower, confusion roiling inside me.

Thirty minutes later I was sitting on the end of my bed, distracting myself by scrolling through photos of the house I'd bought, the house I'd hoped to share with Tess someday. Eventually, Juliet came to knock at the door.

I opened it, and realized that what stood there on the threshold of the bedroom I occupied was pretty much every American man's red-hot fantasy. Juliet Manchester, glowing and gorgeous, in an emerald off-the-shoulder dress that perfectly matched her green eyes, stood waiting for me. Her skin was smooth and perfect, milky and beautiful, and her platinum hair fell in cascading waves over her shoulders. She looked every bit the movie star she was, and I wished for a few minutes I could make this all easier and find myself attracted to her.

But as she stepped near to tell me quietly she'd just heard from her lawyer again, another door opened and Tess stepped out. Over Juliet's head, I watched her emerge from her room and stop, her light hazel eyes wide as she saw us there in my doorway, Juliet leaning in close, one of her hands on my arm.

Tess wore a simple dress, a straight rust-colored silk sheath that hugged her curves but not too tightly. The color was like burnished gold, and it set off gold strands in her hair and lit her skin with a glow I wanted to be near, to feel. Her lips were plump and pink and perfect, and every part of my body and mind responded to her as she met my gaze.

This. This wasn't a dream, it wasn't a misplaced fantasy. I was supposed to be with this woman. I knew it with a certainty I'd never felt about anything.

But right now I couldn't be. Right now I had a job to do.

Tess looked between Juliet and me for a long second, then sighed and turned, walking away as Juliet leaned in closer, bracing her hand on my chest as she finished quietly describing the article that had evidently been published on one of the trashier Hollywood news sites. An article Zac had clearly paid for, which detailed all of Juliet's affairs.

"It'll be okay," I told her, wishing she could have told me all this from just a few feet away. I knew what it must've looked like to Tess—Juliet and I pressed together in the doorway of my room. And I knew I needed to talk to her, to reassure her, to make it clear how I felt about her.

"I really don't see how it will be okay," Juliet sniffed as we turned to head downstairs.

"Because it's not true," I said. "Maybe all the public needs to know, all anyone needs to know, is the truth."

"Zac will ruin me," she said quietly. "The tape ... I can't ..."

I stopped her on the stairs and turned her to face me. "Juliet. You are a good person. In the end, isn't that what really matters? Doesn't that matter more than what the public believes? More than what Zac sells them about you?"

"Maybe you've forgotten what our lives are about," she said. "In our line of work, it doesn't matter what's true. It only matters what people believe."

"We're in a shitty line of work," I said, feeling the darkness in my words settle on my face, drape my shoulders.

"Smile, lovebirds!" Alison was waiting like a vulture at the bottom of the stairs, which were lit brilliantly by the photographers' lights switching on so they could capture our descent. "How about a kiss?"

Juliet leaned in, and though every cell in my body screamed at me not to, I pulled her close and kissed her for the cameras.

"That was perfect," Alison cooed as we descended the rest of the way.

"It was," Tess agreed, her voice coming from the shadows behind the photographer's bright lights. As they switched off the lights to move them, I found her standing in the doorway to the kitchen. "It was perfect," she said, her voice flat and dull.

I didn't know if she was talking about the kiss, or about what had happened between us the day before.

"Tess," I whispered, moving close to her. "I need to talk to you."

"Ryan! Juliet!" Alison called to us as the crew moved out toward the back porch. I glanced in the direction from which Alison's voice had come, then turned back to Tess, torn.

"You should go," Tess said, looking beyond me to the ever-perky Alison, and then she turned, heading back into the kitchen, where the catering staff flitted from place to place like butterflies. I watched her go, her perfect form moving away from me as my heart sank.

Two hours later, the party was in full swing. Well-dressed locals meandered over the rolling green bank of the back lawn, glasses in hand, as waiters passed among the guests wielding silver trays filled with dainty hors d'ouevres.

Alison and the camera crew dogged every move Juliet and I made, and I was beginning to feel more like a crime suspect than a movie star. Every time I turned around, one of them was there, waiting to catch any remotely interesting action on film, to overhear a romantic tidbit shared between my fake girlfriend and me.

They were certainly disappointed, because I was quickly learning that either due to the stress and strangeness of the situation, or because of simpler, biochemical causes, Juliet and I didn't have much to say to one another.

"Tess looks happy at least," she said at one point, sending my gaze back across the lawn to the front of the big tent where Tess was standing with the tall man I'd seen kiss her earlier. I hadn't noticed him returning, and I wasn't pleased to see him now, standing there in his too-short suit and staring at Tess like she made the sun rise.

Maybe she did. I didn't really blame him.

And Juliet was wrong, I thought. Tess was smiling, but she wasn't happy. I wasn't sure how I knew, but I just knew. There was a tightness around the corners of her smile, a hesitancy in her posture as the tall man leaned in to say something next to her ear. I might have known her only a few short days, but Tess was the one thing in the world that made sense to me, the one thing I knew I understood. And I hated seeing her fake happiness almost as much as I hated faking it myself.

Watching him close to her perturbed me. No, that wasn't it. It infuriated me. I wanted to stride over there, yank him away from her and demand that he never touch her again.

Which would have been insane, but what about this weekend hadn't been? Between my sudden heartsick love over a girl I couldn't have, Gran's not-so-subtle jabs at everyone, a lovesick house-chicken…the weekend had been weird. Insane, really. Punching out a stranger would fit right in.

"Who is that guy?" I asked Juliet, pleased when the question came out interested instead of crazy.

"Oh, that's Tony Myers. He and Tess have had a thing, like, forever."

Jealousy leapt into my gut, a green-eyed horned imp with a thirst for vengeance. "A thing?" What kind of thing?" That question came out much closer to crazy, and Juliet side-eyed me.

She waved her hand in the air. "They dated forever ago. He's still hanging on." She narrowed her gaze at me. "Why? Do you think whatever's between you two could be … serious?" I couldn't tell if she sounded concerned or just curious. Either way, she didn't sound happy.

"Do you think she likes him?" I hated that the question sounded like something I would have asked in fifth grade and even more insane than the last one. And then I made it worse. "Like, *likes him* likes him?"

Juliet laughed, but her words didn't reassure me. "I think she likes him enough. He's local," she said. "And eventually they'll probably end up together. It just makes sense."

It didn't make sense to me. Tess didn't love him. I could see that across the wide space between us. I had a sudden urge to sweep in, rescue her, cameras be damned. "That's ridiculous."

"Tess is a local girl," Juliet went on. "She's never had big plans, never wanted to leave here."

"That doesn't mean he's the right guy for her."

Juliet turned to face me, her posture more relaxed than it had been all night, and her interest in whatever I might say clear. The camera crew noticed her sudden shift, and flashes strobed as she stepped in even closer. "You *do* think there's something serious going on with my sister," she said, her eyes widening.

"Not that I can do anything about it with the vultures here," I said, wishing I hadn't voiced my regret aloud as I watched Juliet's face morph from amused to sad. She let out a sigh.

"I'm sorry, Ryan. For all of this." She said the words to me, but looked over my shoulder at the security team next to the tent entrance as she spoke. She really did look sorry in that instant, like this pretense was every bit as difficult for her as it had become for me.

"Come on, movie stars. Time to eat pig and celebrate me not being dead. Tess made a fantastic cake." Gran stepped between us and took each of us by the elbow, dragging us toward the tent where the rest of the crowd was already sitting down and a pit-roasted pig was being paraded in on an extravagant platter.

Wow. That was something you did not see in Los Angeles every day.

Juliet and I were seated at a table across from Tess and Tony, who I was beginning to despise. He was leaning in close to her, kept draping an arm over the back of her chair, and was generally acting as if they were a couple. The guy in my gut poked me a few times with the stick I imagined him holding, trying to prod me into doing something crazy.

While I was essentially being paid to act as if Juliet and I were a couple.

Everything was a disaster.

But it was made impossibly worse when Alison and the camera crew set up on the opposite side of the tent, cameras aimed directly at Juliet and me. There wasn't a moment when I might dare to stare at Tess, or throw a knife at Tony, since it could potentially be caught on camera and would undoubtedly be splashed across the Internet almost instantaneously. We were under a microscope, and I owed it to Juliet to remember that. I'd made her a promise, and she'd been hurt enough. My career wasn't even my focus at this point—I would see this farce through and then… I didn't know what would come next, but more and more I thought there was a different life for me. Waiting here in Maryland. My mind flashed to the other space the real estate agent had shown me—the vacant restaurant on the square in Leonardtown.

"So, you guys … how long have you been together?" It was Tony, leaning across the table to talk to Juliet and me. He waved between us with a steak knife, and I suppressed a shudder. Not that I hadn't used my flatware to converse before, it was just one more thing I could choose to dislike about this guy.

I tried to impale him with tiny daggers fired from my eyeballs as Juliet smiled sweetly at him. "It's new," she said. "Just a few weeks now." She leaned into me and I wrapped my arm around her, rubbing my hand up and down her arm. The motions came naturally, but they felt forced and wrong.

Tess's eyes were on my hand, and I had to keep my heart from leaping out of my chest. It was killing me to know I was hurting her, and the way she was watching us made it clear that despite telling me to stay away, there were feelings there. A tiny hope inside me was trying to elbow Mr. Jealousy out of the way.

"Love in Hollywood," Tony said, grinning. And then he reached for Tess and pulled her into his side. "We kind of have that too, right Tess? Just Hollywood, Maryland."

Tess said nothing, but busied herself with her drink before stealing a glance up at me. Our eyes locked and heat washed through me. This was all so, so wrong.

"So Brian," Tony said, pulling my gaze to his open grinning face. "What was that last movie I saw you in? On an island somewhere or something? Weren't there like zombie islanders?"

I gritted my teeth, reminding myself that I was being filmed. I had to be nice. Or at least I could not leap across the table, remove the bright red apple from the pig's mouth and shove it into Tony's. "*Pacific Pandemic*," I said.

"Ho, ho, yeah," Tony said, laughing and shaking his head of too-shaggy dark hair. "That's destined to be a cult classic, right man? Like way over the top stupid silly."

"It was a horror thriller," I said through my teeth. "The studio's answer to *World War Z*."

Tony guffawed some more and stuffed some corn in his mouth. Then he continued to insult my career. "Brian, man," he leaned in conspiratorially. "So when you're in the middle of making a flop like that, do the actors know it? Or do you like, think things are going really well? Like you know you're standing in a pile of shit, right? But you sign a contract or whatever, so you have to do it, right?" Juliet squeezed my hand, which helped slow down the angry rushing blood that was about to send me over the table to strangle Tony.

Tess was staring at Tony with her own mouth hanging open slightly, and she punched him in the upper arm as he finished this question. I opened my mouth to answer, but Juliet saved me.

"Tony," Juliet said sweetly. "Hollywood is complicated, and sometimes we do movies we know won't be blockbusters for strategic reasons. To get to know a director, or to be connected to another actor. It's hard to explain. And it's not Brian. It's Ryan. Ryan McDonnell is going to be a household name pretty soon. He's moving on to much bigger things," she added. "Right, babe?"

Juliet held my hand tightly and she leaned close, clearly wanting me to kiss her now, to make this good for the ever-vigilant cameras. I appreciated her help with the d-bag, but my mind was a whir. My whole body was reaching for Tess, and her wide hazel eyes were so sad I felt like my heart was dissolving inside my chest. Had I done that to her?

I felt like whatever I did here was a choice laid out in front of me: Continue to go along with this charade, watching Tess being groped by some moronic redneck ex-boyfriend from her past, or stand up right here and tell her what I wanted, what I hoped, what I knew we could have.

But before I could make my choice, Tess abruptly stood.

"Excuse me." She turned and left the tent without another word, and Tony shrugged, returning his attention to the mountain of shredded pork on his plate.

I nearly stood to go after her, but then the DJ turned up the volume and Juliet pulled me out of my seat. "We'd better dance, put on a good show."

Sadness floated inside me as I followed her to the dance floor, every cell in my body screaming to head the other way, to follow Tess from that tent.

Tony must've heard my body's message because a few minutes later, he wiped his mouth, stood, and headed out the door of the tent, as my mind darkened.

CHAPTER TWENTY
TESS

It wasn't the mature thing to do. It wasn't the right thing, considering this was Gran's party. It wasn't an even vaguely advisable thing to do, but I left the party. I stood up and walked out.

I couldn't take one more second of watching Juliet and Ryan fawn over one another like the happy couple they were pretending to be. Were they even pretending? How could I trust a man who lied for a living when he told me it was all for show? How could I trust my sister's words when her job was exactly the same? They were both too good at it, and I'd seen the way men fell for my sister for far too long. And that kiss on the lawn. That hadn't been pretend. No one was that good an actor.

And then I'd seen them coming out of his room earlier.

I didn't know Ryan McDonnell at all. He was an actor, and evidently a much better one than I'd realized. He was playing me, having both the Manchester sisters. I wondered if he and Juliet had a much more complicated deal than the one they'd told me about.

Even if Ryan had felt something for me—and honestly, that

was unlikely given the amount of time he'd known me, and considering the Juliet-Manchester effect—it was probable that Juliet was the only Manchester girl in his heart now. She charmed everyone. Without even meaning to.

What started out as pretending might have evolved. She had that effect on people. On men. And it looked like Ryan had fallen under the spell. Just like every man who'd ever been interested in me—but then met my sister—besides Tony. A flat acceptance landed with a thud in my gut. I'd end up with Tony. He loved me, at least. But could I ever find even a spark of what I'd felt for Ryan with him?

I couldn't think about it now.

I knew I'd have to go back inside. There were speeches to be made. I had to present the cake we'd made to Gran. She deserved everything and I needed to get over my own issues and go celebrate the woman who was parent and best friend to me now.

But I needed a few minutes of fresh air—even if the humidity that suffused Maryland's signature evening atmosphere was pretty far from refreshing. I stood on the riverbank and looked out across the water.

This was home. This was grounding for me. This water, this land. This was where I belonged and what I was made of. And I'd forgotten it for a while in the grip of a wildly intoxicating fantasy. But I remembered it now.

Ryan McDonnell and Juliet would go back to Hollywood tomorrow, and I could go back to kayaks and calm. But I was pretty sure I'd never be settling down with Tony, no matter what everyone seemed to expect. He didn't deserve a woman who didn't love him.

I'd opened my mind for the evening, tried to give him a chance. But there was just nothing there, no more than there had been in seventh grade. We were not meant to be together any more than Buffy and Angel were—though we had a lot less of the star-crossed love thing going on. And a lot less blood sucking and general badassery, too.

"Hey there," Tony's voice came from behind me and I turned in the increasing darkness to see his tall form moving in next to me on the shore of the river. His presence was both comforting and depressing, if that was even possible. I was a mess.

"Hey," I returned softly.

Twinkle lights were starting to glow in the trees around us, and the atmosphere would have been romantic, if only ... but no, I needed to stop thinking that way.

"Everything okay?" Tony asked, his long arms crossed awkwardly in front of him. Though Tony had grown into his body, he still had a bit of goofy puppy dog in his mannerisms. I hoped someone would find it charming one day. He deserved to be loved.

"Yeah," I said, turning to face him. "I'm sorry about dashing. I just needed a little air."

"What else?" He asked.

Damn Tony for picking this instant to be insightful enough to realize there was something else going on.

"Nothing," I tried.

"I've known you almost your whole life. I don't think you can lie to me."

I smiled at him, my heart softening. He had. He had known me forever. And I wasn't the sister with the acting genes. "It's just ... Everything feels confusing."

"Everything?"

"Tony," I said slowly, looking up at my old friend. I knew it was time to address the situation between us—give us both permission to look forward instead of behind. "You know there's never going to be anything romantic between us, right?"

He dipped his head for a minute and a sad smile lifted the

corners of his mouth. "I do know that. Was worth a try, though."

Relief washed through me, along with a very platonic love for my old friend, and I looped my arm through his and leaned my head into his shoulder. "So, if you really want to know what's bothering me, it's boy trouble, I guess." It was easier to talk if we both looked out at the constantly flowing river. "It's Ryan."

"Juliet's boyfriend?"

"He's not," I corrected quickly. "Well, maybe he is. They started off pretending, but now I don't really know. It's just …" I trailed off.

"That is confusing."

"I know, I'm sorry." I tugged on his arm and smiled up at his familiar face, taking some comfort in my friend's willingness to be just that. Just what I needed. A friend.

"Well Tess, I can't tell you what to do about that. But I will tell you something else. Three things, actually."

Tony had never been super insightful, so I was surprised he suddenly had three different opinions. I found myself smiling as I said, "Go for it."

"One, I don't care who he is or what he's done, if he can't see the incredible beauty and grace that surround you, he doesn't deserve you. And two, that movie he was talking about was pure shit. I don't care how he spins it, and I'm not sure there's any coming back from what happened in the final season of *Charade of Stones* anyway." He grinned, and my sad heart lifted as I laughed. I hadn't seen the movie—I hated zombies—but everyone had watched *Charade* when it was on five years ago. That was when I'd fallen in love with Ryan in the first place. That and the movie I'd watched on constant repeat.

"Wasn't there a third thing?" I asked.

"Yeah, there is." Tony smiled down at me. "Tonight isn't

about him. It's about that lady who's still sharp as a tack and mean as a pit bull, who's sitting in there waiting for you to make a speech and give her a cake. She told me earlier she didn't give two squirts of piss about the party, but that she couldn't wait to get her hands on the cake. Her words."

I swallowed hard. He was right. This wasn't about me, or Ryan, or Juliet. Tonight was about Gran, and I was standing out here selfishly moping and wasting time. "You're right." I nodded. "You're right. Come on, let's go give Gran her cake."

I held Tony's arm, and we walked together back into the big tent, which was raucous now with the sound of loud music and people laughing. Bodies twirled in bright colors around the dance floor and the entire atmosphere inside felt light and fun. I spotted Ryan and Juliet dancing on the parquet tile and pushed down the knot that tried to rise up in my throat. This wasn't about them. And it wasn't about me or my stupid feelings.

I grinned over at Gran and she gave me a thumbs up, and then tapped her wristwatch and made a circling motion with her finger. Right. Time to get on with it.

I approached the DJ stand and a few minutes later the music faded and people retook their seats.

"Thanks everyone for coming tonight," I began, uncomfortable at first with the microphone in my hand, my own voice booming through the tent, everyone's eyes on me. I wasn't used to being the center of attention. Not in this family.

I took a deep breath and continued. "As you know, we're here tonight to celebrate one very special woman, Helen Hazel Manchester, my grandmother."

Applause erupted around me and I smiled over at Gran, who looked moderately surprised to hear people clapping in her honor.

"Some of you have known my Gran for most of your lives," I continued. "Tommy Dyson," I turned to address a man much too old to still be going by the moniker Tommy. "You told me earlier tonight that Gran had been the principal of your elementary school, that you remembered being marched into her office, sure you'd be expelled for telling your teacher that spelling was for sissies and girls."

Tommy nodded his head, a blush coloring his already ruddy cheeks even darker.

"And when you sat in front of her, Gran shook her head at you and asked you if you didn't realize what the entire point of spelling was in the first place."

The crowd shifted, waiting for the punch line.

"And what was it?" I asked him, walking over to lean the mic down so he could answer.

"She told me it was one of the best ways to make other people feel dumb and told me to start doing the crossword puzzle every morning. I guess she knew I was a little bit of a bully—not that I'm proud of that now," he said. "But she was trying to give me some ammo and make me a smarter kid in the process."

"Did it work?" I asked him.

"I finish the Times crossword every Sunday, and I bet I'd beat most folks in this tent in a spelling test. 'Cept your gran, of course." He stood up then and bowed deep. "Thanks for putting me on the right path, Principal Manchester."

The crowd loved that and Gran's little face wrinkled in an "aw shucks" smile before she batted her hands at everyone, embarrassed at the attention.

"Gran tries to pretend like she doesn't care about people," I said, scanning the crowd and purposely avoiding Ryan's gaze. "She acts like she doesn't really want to get involved in things, like she'd rather just keep to herself. But my Gran is one of the most perceptive and insightful human beings I've ever known.

"When our parents died when I was seven, I didn't like Gran. She was herself—straight to the point and maybe a teeny bit abrasive. She'd been that way since I was tiny. And when Mom and Dad died and she put us in the back seat of her car and told us we'd be living with her, I was terrified. But I'll never forget the way she turned around and looked at us sitting there scared. She stared at us for a couple minutes, remember Jules? And then she said something I'll never forget. She said, 'I'll never be your mom or your dad, and I'll never try to be. Your little hearts are broken right now, and I won't pretend that's going to get better. Your daddy was my baby, and my heart is broken, too. But I'll tell you what we're going to do, the three of us together. We are going to eat a lot of ice cream, play a whole bunch of Monopoly, and have as much fun as we possibly can. Because that's what your folks would have wanted for you. And for me, too."

I wiped at my eyes, wishing that memory didn't always transport me back to my seven-year-old self, feeling so broken and sad there on that big bench seat next to my sister.

"And that's what we've done," I continued. "Gran became our parent, our confidant, our best friend, and our harshest critic. And I can't imagine my life without her. Happy birthday, Gran. We're so lucky to have you."

"Let's eat the cake before the angel of death comes for me, for God's sake!" she called out. I swallowed my sentimental tears and laughed.

I nodded toward the catering staff, and they rolled out the cake Ryan had helped me make. I'd finished it when he'd disappeared earlier in the day to wherever it was he'd gone. It was a Black Forest cake, because that was Gran's favorite. But it was in multiple tiers, and the entire thing was decorated with fondant armor and weapons and World of Warcraft characters I'd found on the Internet.

Gran's face lit up at the sight of it and she clapped her hands together in front of her, standing to blow out the nine candles on top of the cake—one for each decade. The crowd broke into a round of Happy Birthday as the DJ played a track of birthday music over the speakers. I fitted the mic back into the stand at the front of the dance floor and went up to give Gran a hug. I'd done something right, at least, and happiness found a place next to all my sadness and confusion as I hugged her.

"Thank you, Tessy," she said, her eyes shining up at me as I let her go.

My heart squeezed a little bit in my chest. "I love you, Gran," I told her, kissing the top of her head.

I'd let myself get carried away, had become distracted with things that were completely outside my control, and had been ignoring the whole point of this weekend. Gran. My rock. My best friend. My family.

I should have been with her this weekend, and instead, I'd let myself become wrapped up in the trappings of celebrity life. I had allowed myself to fall so easily into the bright lights and promises that went anywhere a certain hot celebrity couple went. And now, as I smiled at my sister and Ryan, I resolved to remember. His hand rested atop hers on the table, and she leaned comfortably into his side. I ignored the little twist of wistfulness that made my stomach churn.

Being jealous of Juliet was exhausting. And useless.

And letting myself believe anything was possible with Ryan was just a symptom of that same old jealousy. He was hers. Real or pretend, he was hers. He came with her, he'd leave with her, and together, they were part of a world I wanted nothing to do with.

I told myself I'd be happy when they were gone again, and sat down to console my aching heart with a huge piece of black forest cake.

CHAPTER TWENTY-ONE
RYAN

I felt, more than saw, the moment when Tess had come back inside the tent. While my body was on autopilot, dancing along to *Uptown Funk* with Juliet, much to the delight of the cameras and Alison Sands, who was furiously scribbling something as she stood at the edge of the dance floor, my mind was laser focused on the door. Where had Tess gone? Was she coming back?

The relief I felt when she had stepped back in with too-tall Tony was like dropping a load of rocks I didn't even know I was carrying. I just wished Tony would go ahead and move on. I didn't like that he shared history with Tess, that he knew things about her I was dying to learn. I didn't like the light in his eyes when he looked at her, the hope he clearly felt. And I didn't like it when she held his arm as if he was providing some kind of support she needed, like right now.

Tony walked Tess to the microphone at the front of the tent, and the music cut off, so Juliet and I went to sit down. And then Tess began her speech.

Juliet might have been the actress in the family, but that didn't mean Tess wasn't well spoken or captivating in her own right. She was incredible—delivering her heartfelt words with perfect timing, confidence, with a shine in her beautiful eyes.

If I had doubted my feelings for her—crazy and too fast as they were—I was certain of them now. I couldn't explain it, and if you'd told me I would ever believe in love at first sight before, I would have told you to fuck right off. But here it was. I loved her. I loved the sweetness she exuded, the grace with which she moved, the gentle smile she gave her Gran. I loved her hesitation when she caught my eye, and I loved her honesty.

Maybe I loved Tess because it was so clear she knew exactly who she was. And that kind of certainty wasn't something you found in folks who spent their days pretending to be other people for a living.

When she finished speaking, I stood without thinking much about a plan. I just needed to talk to her, to be close to her, cameras be damned.

She had just taken a huge bite of cake, and I sank into the vacant seat next to her, feeling Juliet's eyes on me from across the table, watchful and curious.

"Hi," I said.

"Hello Brian," Tess said through her cake, emphasizing the name Tony had given me.

"Funny." I shook my head as Tess lifted a shoulder and turned back to her cake. "Listen, can we talk? Maybe outside?"

She swallowed and looked up at me again, something sparkling in her eyes that gave me hope. But then she killed it. "I don't think that's a good idea."

My heart dropped and disappointment flooded me. No. This could not be over. "Please," I said, hearing an edge of desperation in my voice I didn't like at all.

Tess heard it too, because she looked at me another long minute, our eyes connecting and sending off sparks in my gut.

Then she stood and gave me a quick nod. "Come out a few minutes after me," she said quietly. "I'll be in the barn."

She left then, and hope turned into a lovesick house-chicken inside me, all moony and soft. She was giving me a chance—a chance to tell her how I felt, to convince her not to ignore what I was sure she felt too. I sat there a minute longer, every cell in my body screaming at me to follow her. But she was right, it was smart to wait, not to appear to be dashing outside in pursuit of the wrong Manchester sister.

Just as I stood to go, my heart in my throat, a hand landed lightly on my arm.

"Ryan." It was Alison. "I have a few questions. I thought maybe we could chat for a minute." She sat in the seat Tess had just vacated, and my heart sank to the floor as I slid back into my own seat.

"Sure," I heard myself say, but my mind was already outside, already crossing the wide expanse of lawn, stepping into the big darkened barn. Where Tess was waiting for me.

"Well," Alison began, looking down and turning through pages of notes in a small moleskin book. "So, your last film," she said, still flipping pages. "That was the one most critics are referring to as the *Titanic* of your career, right? With the zombies?"

I hated that reference. There had been memes online with an iceberg covered in zombies and me at the helm of a ship. Because part of it had been set in Antarctica, and I was supposed to be the captain of this research vessel—you get the idea.

"Right."

"So on the heels of that failure, and after everything that happened with *Charade*, how much do you think this new relationship with Juliet Manchester will help?"

I felt my eyes narrow. She had my full attention now. "First of all, I don't know how many years I'll have to apologize for the way *Charade* ended. I mean, everyone knows the actors don't actually write the show, right?" I was so tired of talking about that show, I thought my head would blow off. "Wait, what did you ask after that?"

"I just mean that there is a bit of speculation that the relationship with Juliet is a PR move mostly. I wondered if you could comment on that?" Alison smiled sweetly, and I wondered suddenly if she'd known all along. Did she actually know anything now? My mind raced as I tried to figure out how to spin this to save Juliet.

"Well, you're very savvy, Alison," I said, pasting on a grin. "And you're one-hundred percent right."

"Really?" Alison perched on the edge of her seat, pushing away Tess's cake and leaning toward me.

"I mean, yes. There's no way anyone can be associated with Juliet Manchester and not see their star rise a little. She's a phenomenon." Alison was nodding madly. "Who also happens to be one of the sweetest, most genuine, and kindest people in Hollywood. Not to mention lovely, inside and out."

This wasn't what Alison had wanted to hear. Her posture stiffened. "So this relationship ..."

"Has made me one of the luckiest men alive," I confirmed. It had been luck, after all. It didn't mean I was in love with Juliet, though. But Alison didn't need to know that. "And if my career gets a boost just because I adore Juliet Manchester? Well, that's just gravy, right?" I stood, smiling graciously. "Excuse me."

Alison might have had more questions, or suspicions, but I didn't care. Tess was waiting for me, and my heart wouldn't let me waste another second pretending not to understand exactly what should happen next. I glanced behind me, but Alison was so busy scribbling, she didn't notice me leave.

I slipped out the tent door and made my way around the edge of the sprawling lawn, avoiding the glow of the lights strung in the trees. A few people meandered here and there, appreciating the beauty of the landscape, the water. I didn't need them to see me and strike up a casual conversation, delaying me even more.

The barn door stood open, and I stepped inside, into the dark interior. It was quiet, as if the barn stood in a world apart from the music and light just outside. The faint smell of horses and hay drifted around me, and from the darkness, a familiar voice said, "Hi." Just the sound of it brought a smile to my face and made a little beat echo through my body.

My eyes adjusted slowly, and I found Tess sitting on an overturned crate, her arms resting on her knees. She looked innocent and vulnerable there, and I had to resist the urge to move straight to her, to gather her in my arms.

"Hey," I said, pulling up another crate to sit next to her.

Neither of us spoke for a moment as the sounds from the party outside filtered through the thick warm air, sifting bass beats and high laughing voices into single notes and a vibration I could feel in my bones.

"The party is going so well," I said. "Do you think Gran is enjoying herself?"

"Well, she's still there, as far as I know. That's a good sign." Her voice was soft, uncertain in the darkness.

"Thanks for meeting me out here," I said, trying to pad the way gently into the conversation I wanted to have, though I wasn't sure exactly what to say.

"Sure," she said. "But I only have a second. People will start leaving now that we've had cake. I need to wish them goodnight. I'm the hostess."

"Of course, yeah." I turned toward her, just her outline visible against the light spilling in from the open barn door. "Okay, well." I took a deep breath, trying to still my racing heart, to make sense of the thoughts flying through my mind. "I looked at houses today."

That wasn't quite where I'd hoped to start.

Tess turned to look at me, and even in the dark I could see her eyebrows go up in confusion. "Um. Okay," she said slowly. "Wait, what?"

"To buy. I bought a house here." Closer. Still nonsensical.

Think, Ryan.

This was easier when I had a script.

Tess didn't speak immediately, so I tried again. "I'm going to have a home here. I love it here—the water, the trees. It's so different than any place I've ever been."

"Oh." There was an edge of disappointment there, and I realized I didn't say what I needed to say. "Okay, well …" Tess moved to stand and I caught her hand.

"Wait, please." I held her soft hand between my palms, resisting the urge to bring my mouth to her smooth skin. "It's not just the scenery, Tess. I want to be here to be close to you, to give us a chance."

Tess tugged on her hand, but I didn't let it go, standing to face her instead.

"Ryan, that doesn't make any sense," she said, shaking her head and sounding small and defeated in the darkness. "People don't do things like that. I mean, buy a vacation home, sure, yeah. But you're not going to stay here. You're not going to live here."

"Why not?"

"Because you're Ryan McDonnell!"

My name sounded like a curse on her lips.

"You're a movie star, and women all over the world throw themselves at you. You've got a rising career, you're linked to America's Sweetheart. Southern Maryland has nothing to offer you."

"It has you, Tess." I kept her hand in mine, but lifted my other hand to capture her jaw, to still the shaking of her head. "It has everything I want because it has you."

Happily Ever His

I felt her soften beneath my touch, and though there were more words that needed to be said, more things that had to be cleared up and explained, in the moment, I brought my lips to hers because the universe demanded it, pulling us together like it was meant to be. She melted into my touch, and as our lips met, I felt my future unfurl before me like a long ribbon with no end, undulating in the breeze blowing over the Potomac.

This.

But a second later it was over, the ribbon snapping and sinking beneath the murky water.

"Ryan, no." Tess broke the kiss, pulled herself from my arms. "This isn't right. You're with my sister, and I'm not getting in the middle of all of that. I don't live in the same world you do, and I can't afford to get swept up in movie star fantasies. I'm too old for that. I live in the real world." Her voice broke as she said, "Just stay away from me, and then go home. Go back to Hollywood, where you belong."

She turned and walked out the big barn door, leaving me standing in the dark, my heart racing and my future becoming a distant icon as she moved away from me.

More than ever, I knew exactly what I wanted.

I wanted her, and I didn't care about anything else.

CHAPTER TWENTY-TWO
TESS

I practically ran out of the barn. The last thing I needed was more time in his arms, more ideas blooming in my mind about what might be possible between us. I'd settled myself with reality this afternoon. Movie stars were Juliet's business, not mine. And I wouldn't survive the heartbreak that would come with Ryan McDonnell.

I slid back into my seat next to Granny, ignoring her questioning stare, and shoveled a huge bite of my waiting cake into my mouth.

"Jesus, slow down, Tess," Granny said, cringing at my gluttony. "You've already had a brush with death once today, and I swear to God I'm going first. I'll stab myself with this butter knife if I have to." She picked up a piece of flatware from the table and waved it menacingly as I scarfed down cake.

Hell, if I couldn't have Ryan, at least I could have chocolate and cherries. I closed my eyes and forced myself to enjoy it. Yes. Cake. I would have a future filled with sugary smooth cake and frosting. It would be glorious, and I would just have to get bigger kayaks. And bigger clothes to fully accommodate the true love of my life. Chocolate cake.

Mmmm. I was shoving another mouthful in, telling myself I was fine when I heard Ryan's voice over the speakers.

"I hope you don't mind if I take just a second to say something," he said, and the crowd quieted again.

CHAPTER TWENTY-THREE
RYAN

I hadn't been sure what would happen when I picked up that microphone. I only knew I had to.

"What are you waiting for?" Juliet had asked, shoving me in the ribs with her small hand.

My eyes found hers. "But … the cameras. Alison is on us like Gran on a Manhattan."

Juliet shrugged and her eyes scanned the room. I assumed she was looking to see if Alison was watching, but her gaze moved somewhere else and I followed the direction, but as I turned my head, she laughed lightly and turned back to me. One of her security guards at the tent entrance gave me a light nod and I lifted my hand. I was too nervous to wonder what that was all about. At his side, Jack and the chicken stood, the chicken wearing a little bow tie for the party.

I thought it was a girl chicken. I guessed girls could wear bowties too.

"I'm sick of pretending," Juliet finally said, pulling me back from my chicken ponderance. "And I don't think it makes things better. Mostly, I think it hurts the people we care about."

"If we stop pretending," I reminded her, "the press goes

back to pulling apart the details of your divorce. They'll find out about the settlement. The tape."

"They'll find out anyway." Her voice was tired, resigned. "It's like trying to stop a tidal wave with a silk scarf, Ryan. In the long run, it's impossible. And really … what's the worst that could happen?"

"The scarf would be wrecked," I quipped. I was still considering her question, knowing full well the worst that could happen would happen to Juliet, not to me. My agent might be disappointed. My career might not explode as we'd hoped, but my agent was going to be plenty disappointed anyway, when I let her know I was planning to relocate to Maryland. What difference would this make? Juliet went on.

"Please put my sister out of her misery," she said. "Look at her, she's so consciously trying not to look at you, it's hurting *me*. And I think she might be trying to commit suicide via cake."

"She is?"

"Oh my God, do I need to do this for you guys?" Juliet started to stand up.

"No, no." I pulled her back down and was surprised when the burly security guard who'd been by the door was suddenly standing behind us.

"Easy," he growled. I released Juliet, looking between them. What was going on here?

"It's fine," Juliet said, glancing up at him, something soft in her eyes. "Jace, I'm fine."

The mountain of man backed off and I raised an eyebrow at Juliet. "Pretty devoted security there."

She ignored my comment. "Do I need to tell my sister how you feel?"

"No," I said. "No, of course not."

A minute later, I had the microphone in my hand and was running my mouth, wishing I'd planned out something to say.

My stomach was in my throat and my palms were so sweaty I had to keep switching hands and rubbing them across my tux, but somehow I managed to get out the words I needed.

They were crazy words—even to my own ears. I wasn't just talking when I said I'd never believed in love at first sight. What an insane idea. Love involves time and experience, shared hardship and a deep chemical attraction, right? How could anyone possibly believe they loved someone else the second they first saw them? It sounded impossible.

But I knew for a fact it wasn't. It was real. It wasn't like my rational mind looked at Tess Manchester and said, "yep, that one."

But still, I knew it was true.

CHAPTER TWENTY-FOUR
TESS

"Hi everyone," Ryan began as the cake turned to cement in my mouth. "I've gotten to meet a few of you here tonight, and maybe a couple of you know me a little bit from before tonight." A low chuckle rumbled through the crowd. They knew who Ryan McDonnell was. Half the women in the tent had cocktail napkins and pens sitting in front of their dinner plates, trying to work up the nerve to ask him for an autograph.

"Anyway, I'm Ryan, and the first thing I wanted to say is happy birthday, Helen." He turned and smiled at Gran, who had dropped her knife and was grinning at him and eating her cake, watching this unexpected spectacle. She gave him a quick thumbs up, and I watched Ryan take a deep breath, seem to force his broad shoulders down, and turn to look back at the crowd.

"Quit it," I hissed at her. "You're not on his side."

"His side?" she looked at me questioningly.

God, he was handsome. I wished I didn't notice.

But it didn't hurt anything just sitting here appreciating, right?

Eating cake, looking at handsome men. Those things were harmless.

I'd noticed the way he looked earlier, of course. But now I could openly appreciate it. The tux fit him perfectly, the jacket hitting him just high enough to appreciate the way his waist narrowed into lean hips and that perfect round ass. His jacket hugged his arms and shoulders, rippling as he moved and leaving no doubt about the sheer strength of the body beneath. A body I'd gotten to run my hands over, trace my mouth across. I squeezed my eyes shut hard and tried not to remember.

It was impossible, and my body heated at just the memory of his stubble grazing the sensitive skin along my collarbone.

"I also wanted to thank you all for welcoming me here. The Manchester family especially. Juliet, of course, and Tess." He looked at me then, and when our eyes met, an electric zing jolted through me. I'd been avoiding making eye contact with him all night. Especially since returning from the barn. Now that I had, I knew why I had to avoid it. I hoped I'd still be able to walk straight.

"I've never been to Maryland before," he went on. "Never really even considered the place, if you want the truth. I grew up out west, and my education probably wasn't what it could have been. Will you all hate me if I tell you I never knew Maryland had beaches?" He shrugged as a few people laughed. "I knew about the crabs." He delivered this line looking right at me, and I felt my cheeks heat, but made sure not to let my eyes meet his for more than a glance.

As the crowd shifted in their seats, I wondered what the hell he was doing. Was he really this much of a diva that he needed to commandeer the microphone at an old lady's birthday party? But then he started in a different direction.

"Most of you here have been told I came to Maryland with

Juliet. That's true. At least in one sense. We did fly out here together. We've been working together, and our agents thought it would be a good idea for us to spend more time together off set. That kind of thing is good for the movie. I suggested to Juliet it would be even better if people thought we were together—like, as a couple."

The crowd murmured and a burst of shock ran through me. It hadn't been his idea. She'd told me her agent orchestrated the whole thing. Why was he lying?

"That kind of falseness is part of our business, I guess. My agent thought it was a great idea, good for my career especially. And Juliet was sweet enough to invite me to join her here to celebrate her grandmother's birthday party. So I came along.

"I thought I'd hang out, meet some people, pretend to be dating Juliet Manchester and then go back to LA with a bright and shiny newly buoyant career. I hoped for all that really, because I honestly haven't really ever hoped for anything else. Hollywood saved me from some of the things that weren't great in my life, gave me things I'd never dreamed I'd have. But I think it takes some things from us, too." He looked at Juliet, and she nodded at him.

I watched her a beat longer, and had the sense she had just given him some kind of silent permission, her approval.

"So when I got here and met a woman who made me reevaluate everything I thought I knew about the world, about myself, about what was possible and what I thought I wanted … well, I didn't expect any of it.

My heart raced and I glanced at my sister, who looked perfectly fine with this little speech. He was going to out them? What would happen to her? At the same time, my skin warmed with the knowledge he was talking about me, talking to me, and my desire to know what he'd say next overwhelmed my worry for my sister.

"And when she allowed me time to know her a little bit, time to explore this amazing place and to imagine a life that didn't include fake relationships, a security detail, and a magazine reporter scribbling your every word on a tablet—" he paused and most of the crowd turned to look at Alison Sands, who was too busy scribbling his every word into a tablet to notice. "Well, Tess Manchester let me dream with her just a little bit. And the funny thing is, I don't think any of it was a dream. I think what you people have here, this place, this life—this is the real world. And what you have here, whether you know it or not—getting to be this close to Tess Manchester every single day? I'd trade anything for it."

My heart was skittering unsteadily, a mix of embarrassment and confusion rising inside me. I didn't like being the center of attention, and the whole room was looking at me now, wondering what the hell Ryan was talking about. *I* wondered what the hell he was talking about. Because I didn't dare to hope that whatever he'd been trying to say in the barn could actually have been real.

"Tess," he said, crossing the room to stand just next to where I sat. My heart pounded and I felt my cheeks flame as hope blossomed inside me. He reached down and took my hand, pulling me to my feet. He lowered the microphone a bit and turned me to face him, so we were standing face to face, the mic between us. It was obvious he'd handled a microphone before, an advantage of his background, I supposed. I still couldn't bring myself to meet his eyes, so I stared at his bow tie instead. It was an emerald green, like my sister's dress. "Tess," his voice was softer now, but still projected through the silent tent. "I'm so sorry about all the pretense, the acting … about it all."

Someone in the crowd called out, "You should apologize for the way *Charade of Stones* ended!"

I stifled a laugh.

Who knew we had hecklers in Southern Maryland? But I couldn't disagree with the sentiment.

Ryan shook his head, smiling in an apologetic way, like he agreed with the heckler. "Maybe I deserved that. But it wasn't the acting there, right?" He looked around, chuckling, but then turned his focus back to me. "Still, about the acting. I can't do it anymore, but not just because it was a bad idea in the first place and it never felt right. But because it isn't fair to you. Or to my heart.

"I'm falling in love, Tess." The crowd rustled in excitement, and I just stood there, not breathing, not looking at his face as he talked to me, inches away, everything in my body hanging on his next word. He took my hand again, where it hung at my side, and the warmth of his rough thumb rubbed over the top of my fingers, making my knees actually wobble. "I'm falling in love with Maryland, and with a life that includes crabs and rivers and miles of cornfields. But mostly, I'm falling in love with you."

The room was silent, except that I thought people could probably hear my heart galloping loudly in my chest. I sucked in a breath and looked up, meeting his warm beautiful eyes.

"I bought a house," he said, more quietly.

"You said that before. But I don't understand." This didn't seem to fit with the rest of his speech.

"That's what I was trying to tell you before. Here. I bought a house here. I'm going to stay."

I could feel my head shaking, but I didn't remember deciding to shake it. He couldn't stay here. He was a movie star. And I thought he'd probably actually fallen in love with my sister. None of this made any sense.

"What about Juliet?" I asked in a whisper.

"She'll be okay."

"No, I mean … don't you love Juliet?" It might have been dense, but I needed to hear it. Every boy I'd ever loved had loved Juliet. The idea that this one—this perfect man who I'd worshipped much longer than I was comfortable admitting—might choose me first? It just seemed impossible.

He laughed, a low rumble that twisted up my insides and made me want to lean my head into his chest to hear it better. "No, silly. I love you. Since the moment I first saw you—and I've never believed in love at first sight. But I love you, Tess. Only you. And I want to stay here, if you'll let me."

I was still shaking my head, but now I heard myself laugh incredulously. "If I'll let you?"

"Let me stay. Let me take you out on a real date. On a bunch of real dates. Be my girlfriend. Maybe one day … be my wife?"

My mind exploded in sparks at the thought of marrying Ryan, and something inside me—my soul, maybe?—whispered *yes. Yes.*

The crowd erupted into applause, and for a second I thought maybe he had a ring hidden in his tux somewhere, but I was relieved when he didn't produce one. All of this was overwhelming—I'd known him three whole days, after all. A ring would have been actual insanity.

"Will you?" he asked, and the tent quieted again.

I stared up at him, everything in my body already screaming yes. "Will I …?"

"Will you let me stay? Will you let me show you every day how perfect we can be together, how perfect our lives will be?"

"I don't want perfect," I said, not really thinking about the words first. His face fell, and I quickly added, "I want real."

He nodded, understanding lighting his eyes. "Can I stay?"

I smiled up at him. "Please," I managed. "Please stay." It was a whisper, but the tent heard it and everyone jumped to their feet, applauding. Ryan put the microphone on the table and slid his arms around me, pulling me into his warm firm body and pressing the softest, sweetest kiss to my lips. It was a kiss that whispered promises and futures. It was a kiss that showed me cozy nights and snuggly sexy mornings. It was the kiss I'd dreamed of my whole life.

CHAPTER TWENTY-FIVE
RYAN

Tess wanted me to stay.
As she said the words, her eyes shining and fixed on mine, her arms reaching for me, my heart filled and something like warm chocolate flowed through my veins, comfort and hope and excitement all mixing to produce a feeling of happiness like nothing I'd ever known.

And when I kissed her in that tent, in front of the crowd, when I revealed the truth that had been in my heart since the day I'd seen Tess Manchester, my world snapped into alignment. Tess was everything I wanted. I knew she was right for me.

But it was more existential than that. It wasn't my mind, or my body—though they were both involved—it was deeper. It wasn't even my heart, I didn't think. It sounded completely batty, but I was pretty sure it was my soul that identified a partner in Tess the second I saw her.

I'd been with women, I'd dated plenty. And I'd never before felt that instant of revision. I'd never before experienced the sensation that because this person, this singular individual, had stepped into my path, nothing in my life would ever be the same. But I knew it was possible, because I'd felt it happen with Tess.

"I love you, Tess."

They were the easiest, truest words I'd ever spoken, and I didn't care if everyone else thought I was nuts.

When I held her in my arms after that perfect, amazing, soul-clenching kiss, as the crowd erupted around us, she'd whispered, "I love you, too." And I worried I might combust from the perfection of it all.

"Ryan?" A voice interrupted the perfect moment, and I looked over my shoulder to find Alison and the camera crew crowded between the tables, practically drooling. "A couple questions?"

Even with everything I wanted in my arms, my heart fell as I realized what the next few minutes would mean for Juliet. "Sure," I said. "Let's step outside."

Tess squeezed my hand and I led the magazine crew out to the back porch as the party picked back up and the DJ started playing 90s rap, evidently Gran's favorite, because I heard her thin voice start in with "This here's a tale for all the fellas…"

LATER, I sat with the Manchester girls on the back porch of the huge old plantation house, the tent dark and silent and the guests and cameras finally gone home. A warm calm surrounded us as I held Tess's hand and we stared out into the twinkling lights still sparkling in the trees.

"It was a good party, girls," Gran said. "Plenty of drama, good food, and that cake was amazing, Tess."

Tess's beautiful face glowed with the praise. "Thanks, Gran. I'm glad you had a good time."

"I guess I have to be ninety now." Gran sounded peeved.

"How exactly will that change anything?" Juliet asked.

"Meh," Gran said lightly. "I might have to start taking fiber supplements or something. Maybe get one of those buttons in case I fall and I can't get up."

Juliet and Tess exchanged a look over Gran's head as I chuckled.

"I think you're doing fine," Juliet said, laying her hand on the old woman's.

The river beyond the banks was sparkling with moonlight, the cicadas buzzing low and constant around us. Summer here felt alive in a way it never had out west, definitely not in Los Angeles. I loved it.

"Tired?" Tess asked me after a few moments of contented silence.

I faked a yawn. "I am, actually."

"Oh for God's sake, you don't have to pretend," Gran said. "Go on upstairs, you two." I should have been embarrassed that everyone here knew exactly why Tess and I were both eager to get upstairs, to be alone. But I wasn't. My heart, my mind…my soul were too full for any other emotion to weasel its way in. I was happy—maybe for the first time in my life.

"Don't be loud," Juliet said, her voice a pleading whine.

I took Tess's hand in mine and said goodnight quickly to Gran and Juliet before practically pulling Tess up the stairs.

At the top of the stairs I hesitated, not sure which room we should head into, and part of me still suffered some disbelief that she was mine to take anywhere. Instead of manhandling her into a bedroom and then pinning her beneath me against a wall, I pulled her to my chest and looked down into her eyes, shining in the darkness.

"I can't believe I get to hold you," I said, wishing my words were more eloquent, more right.

"I can't believe you said all those things in the tent and I didn't get to say a word," she said.

A tiny trickle of panic tried to work its way through me.

She was right—I'd done all the talking. I'd said 'I love you' and we'd barely gotten to speak after that. I'd gone to talk to the magazine and she'd joined me after a few minutes, but we hadn't had a moment alone since then. "You can say whatever you want to now," I said.

I could barely see her in the darkness, but the sliver of reflected light shining off the hardwood floor of the hall reflected onto her face enough for me to know her pretty face transformed into a wicked grin, and she pulled me into her bedroom and shut the door behind us.

"Sit down," she commanded, turning on a lamp next to the bed that cast the room in a warm pink glow that reminded me of her, of pure femininity, of softness and home. "Take off your shirt."

My skin tingled, my body began to buzz and my cock jumped to attention immediately. I liked where this was going. But I hoped to hear her repeat my words again, if only because I'd never said them to anyone before and there was a sliver of childish doubt trying to work its way into my newfound happiness.

When my shirt was in a pile next to the bed, Tess knelt between my legs and reached for my belt as I watched her hands, my body flooding with want.

I inhaled sharply as her slim white fingers grazed my abdomen and she worked on my belt buckle. I watched, unable to tear my eyes away from her hands, so close to me. She pulled the belt out, loop by loop and held it in her hands as she stood back up. There was something mischievous in her smile, and for a second I wondered if she planned to smack me with the belt. A tiny jolt of excitement spiked inside me, but then she turned and let the belt slip from her hands.

"Now that you've got me here, what do you plan to do with me?"

"You'll see," she said, looking over her shoulder at me, her hair falling down her back just above that perfect round ass. My body was thrumming and all I wanted was to pull her down on me, to feel every inch of her with my hands, my mouth … my … everything.

She went around the room, tidying things up as my body screamed for action, or for words at least. "Tess, I—"

"I'm thinking," she said suddenly, turning back to face me. "It's just … I … Ryan, this all happened so fast. And I'm trying to work out how much of it I can trust."

"I had to take my shirt off for that?"

"It helps me think," she said, grinning as she turned to face me.

"I can take my pants off too," I offered.

She rolled her eyes.

"You can trust all of it, Tess." I stood, but something about her posture, her straight back, her crossed arms, made me stand still. "I meant all of it."

"And I believe you. Or I want to. I just … I don't trust me, my own heart, I guess."

"Why?" I asked, taking a slow step forward. If she still had doubts, I had every intention of holding her close, of proving my love to her with every inch of myself until they'd been banished. "What is it saying?"

A half-smile lifted one side of her mouth and her eyes widened. God, I wanted to hold her. But I held back, approaching slowly, trying not to spook her.

"It's telling me to run into your arms, to bury my head in your chest, to hold onto you as tightly as I can and to stay there as long as you'll let me." She dropped my gaze immediately after saying these words. "It's saying I love you, and it scares the shit out of me."

"I love you," I said simply, my heart pounding so loudly I thought they could probably hear it downstairs.

She shook her head and laughed. "This just … It doesn't happen like this, right? In three days?"

I shrugged. "It did for me."

The hazel eyes flickered across mine and then dropped again. "For me too."

"Tess," I said softly, and she looked up then, meeting me fully in the eye. "Come here."

She hesitated, lingering a minute more by the soft pink chair in the corner, and then I watched the hesitation fall from her face like a mask, and she rushed into my arms, her hands sliding up my back and pressing hard against me as my skin caught fire again.

Her body was perfect against mine, hot and supple and soft, and I found the zipper holding her inside the rust-colored sheath, dropping it to the ground around her ankles without letting her go. A tiny whimper escaped her as the dress fell, and I swept her up into my arms, carrying her to the bed, where I laid her before me in her purple lace panties and strapless bra. "Perfect," I might have said aloud.

She smiled then, a happy look that telegraphed her acceptance of this crazy truth, her belief that three days could be enough, that they could be the beginning of forever. I straddled her hips and her hands found the button of my pants, unfastening it and pushing them down over my hips. I stood again to rid myself of them, and my boxer briefs, and then slid back on top of her.

I leaned forward, taking her mouth with mine as her hands searched my body, leaving little lines of fire everywhere they touched me. Her tongue was sweet and eager, sliding against mine hungrily, and I had to break off the kiss as she arched beneath me, worried I might ruin it all much too fast. She was too perfect, too… everything.

I moved to drop kisses along the column of her throat below

her ear instead, trailing them down to her collarbone, to the plump swell of her chest. She reached behind herself, arching as she took off her bra, and tossed it aside. Her hands moved to the sides of her chest, pressing her breasts up toward my seeking tongue, and the sight of her hands on her own body nearly sent me over the edge. I covered her hands with mine and took one nipple in my mouth, my body singing as she rewarded me with a breathy moan. My thumb flicked the tight peak of the other breast as I sucked and swirled the one in my mouth, and then I switched. Tess moaned, sending another flare of excitement through me.

My hands slipped along her body, tracing lines and curves, learning every inch of her, and I slid down the bed, pulling off the lacy panties as I went. Every inch of me throbbed at the promise of her sweetness, and I slid back up her body, meeting her glazed eyes.

I leaned down, searching the floor for my pants, for the condom I kept in my wallet, and sighed with relief when I located it, Tess's wide eyes on me the whole time, and her hands playing tantalizing rhythms across my skin.

I rolled on the condom and Tess watched, her eyes taking in every detail, and then her hands reached for me. Her tight hot hand fisted around me and she pulled me near, guiding me with my own dick like a pet she had tamed. I sucked in a sharp breath at her touch—I loved it.

She slid her hand softly over my length, a teasing touch through the latex skin of the condom, and then she dropped her other hand into her own folds, and a shot of sheer need ricocheted through me.

In a breathy voice filled with promise and vulnerability, she said, "I love you, Ryan." And then, as she slid me into her depths, her eyes closing as I pressed home, she added, "I just can't believe I'm in bed with Ryan fucking McDonnell."

The laugh that came from my chest was genuine and happy, and I pulled out a bit and drove back to the hilt to make her point. I was Ryan fucking McDonnell, and I was currently fucking the woman of my dreams.

"I'm yours, Ryan fucking McDonnell," she said, her eyes on mine, and a smile on her beautiful face. Less certainly, she said, "Keep me forever."

In that moment, it was the most romantic thing I'd ever heard. "I will," I promised, knowing I'd never let her go.

EPILOGUE

TESS

"Tess?" Gran called from her lair, which had been reestablished in the sunny parlor at the front of the house.

I stepped in, wiping my hands on my apron. "You paged me?"

She shook her head, laughing. "I'm out of Rye. Can you ask that nice boy to pick some up today?"

"God forbid you can't make a Manhattan at exactly five o'clock," I chided playfully. "But yes, I'll ask the nice boy. And his name is Ryan, Gran."

"I know that."

Once the party had ended and life had gone back to a semblance of normal, Gran had become grumpier than usual, and it had taken me a week or so to figure out why.

In some ways, it had been the best week of my life. Ryan fucking McDonnell really did move here. He'd bought a house by the water, and had arranged to have his things sent and he was going back soon to get his father and bring him here.

His dad wasn't doing well, and the nurse Ryan had hired had helped him vet the community Gran had pointed him to, agreeing that it was a good fit. Mr. McDonnell would be living nearby, and Ryan had made peace with the idea of him living apart, in a place where he had round the clock care. And unlike the extremely costly community in Santa Monica that Ryan had been considering, this one was affordable.

In the meantime, he'd furnished part of the house from the local shops, and had a wonderful bedroom and a functioning kitchen set up in the new place. We'd spent long evenings on his huge deck and even longer mornings in his big bed. But Gran had seemed frailer suddenly, and we spent most of our time at the plantation house with her.

Finally, I'd sat down with her, worried. "Gran, what's going on?"

She had shaken her head like a child, refusing to look me in the eye.

I began to guess. "You're sad because you're ninety and now you actually feel like you're aging?"

A head shake.

"You're bummed because the party's over and Jules went home?"

Another shake.

"Is it Chessy? You miss Chessy?" Jack had called a week after he'd gotten home, and confided that he really missed his chicken friend. He'd asked if there was any chance he might drive out and adopt her, and Gran had agreed. Chessy had been moping since he'd left anyway.

"It isn't the damned chicken," Gran said.

"You're acting like a child."

An angry glare.

Ryan walked by the window outside, shirtless after a run. I stared at him, still shocked that he kept coming back, that it hadn't all turned out to be just a really amazing, really lucid dream.

We both watched until he was out of sight, and something occurred to me.

"Wait, Gran," I said softly. "Are you upset that Ryan stayed here?"

She lifted a shoulder, still not giving in.

"You're not happy for me?" This seemed hard to believe. She'd told me forever to find someone to make me happy. "You're—?" I was about to try again, but she finally opened her mouth.

"I don't want you to leave me, okay? I just … I'm too old to live by myself." She stared down at her lap as she said it, and I thought my strong old Gran looked closer to tears than I could ever remember seeing her. "Everyone in my life has left me, Tess. Everyone but you. My son—your handsome father—is gone. My husband has been gone for more years than I can even believe. All my friends have died." She looked up at me then, and I saw the years on her face, saw how lonely it was to be ninety and feel alone.

"No," I said softly. "I'll never leave you, Gran. Never." I pulled her into my arms, leaning forward and wrapping myself around her. We weren't very affectionate normally, but I held her thin body close and tried to push all my love for her through that hug. "I'm not going anywhere," I whispered.

Gran pulled back and shook herself slightly, like a cat throwing off irritating drops of water. "But that's silly to promise, isn't it? You're young. You're in love. It's selfish of me to make you feel guilty about it." She looked up at me then, all the sadness pushed down inside her, replaced by the ninety years of experience she'd gathered.

"Of course not. You're my family. You're all I've got besides Jules. We're sticking together."

"But Ryan bought that house for you."

"He bought a house," I confirmed. "But this is my home."

"Maybe I'll go live in the place Ryan's dad is going to go."

She pushed out her lip as she said it, and I realized that maybe the situation with Ryan's dad had made her consider her own mortality in a more real way.

"Gran," I whispered, forcing her to look me in the eye. "You can live wherever you want. If you want to move there, to one of those cute little cottages we showed Ryan's dad, you can. But his challenges are very different from yours, and you know that."

"If I moved there'd be other old people around. Maybe I'd make some friends."

I nodded, but her words sounded like she was just testing the idea out. "Whatever you want."

Gran's wrinkled face collapsed on itself for the briefest of moments, and a tiny sob escaped her, and then she recovered herself, sucking in a long breath and shaking her shoulders out slightly. "Tess," she said then. "It sucks getting old."

"Better than the alternative?" I suggested.

She winked. "It is."

FOR THE NEXT FEW WEEKS, we all settled into a new normal. Ryan busied himself fixing up the house, and moved some of his stuff into my room at Gran's. I kept a few things at Ryan's, but I meant what I'd said to Gran. I wasn't leaving her. And Ryan understood, making himself equally at home in our place as he was at his own new house. His father became a fixture in our lives too, Ryan picking him up and taking him home whenever he liked, and he and Gran became drinking and card-playing buddies.

Eventually, Gran allowed me to pack her a bag and show her the room we'd set up for her at Ryan's. It was a mother-in-law suite, with a full living room and kitchen just for her.

Ryan had outfitted the living room with the very best

gaming computer he could find, and Gran clapped her hands like a little girl when she saw it. "I might be okay to hang out here sometimes," she told us. "Just for a change of scenery. And to keep Ronald company." She smiled affectionately at Ryan's dad, who smiled back. Ronald didn't speak much, seemed mostly content to go along for the ride. But Gran confided that he told dirty jokes when they were alone, so it was no wonder she liked him.

Some evenings, it was just Gran and I because Ryan was in Leonardtown working on his new restaurant, and on those nights we stayed at her house.

"You think he can actually cook?" Gran asked me one night while we ate a quiet dinner on the back porch of the old house, its quiet wings stretched around us in the fading light.

"He can, and you know it," I reminded her. Since moving, Ryan had made us multiple amazing meals, revealing a talent that went far beyond Black Forest cake.

"But a restaurant..." Gran trailed off, shaking her head.

"It's his dream, Gran."

"It seems a little crazy that his dream wasn't being a movie star. How many dreams can one good looking guy get?"

I just smiled. Ryan had been so happy since he'd gotten the restaurant space set up and the management and kitchen staff hired. He was giving his name and his vision to the place, and cooking one weekend night a week, but otherwise, he was going to be hands-off for the most part.

"He can have as many dreams as he wants," I told her. I was just glad I was one of those dreams.

We were at Ryan's on the back porch about a month after the party, drinking Manhattans in the late summer afternoon, when the magazine arrived.

"Here it is," Ryan said, holding up the glossy magazine with a photo of my sister splashed across the cover in the green dress she'd worn at Gran's party. He handed it to Gran and me, and we leaned together, looking at the cover and Ronald nodded, maybe not quite understanding but happy enough just to be with us all.

In a smaller box on the cover was a photo of Ryan, holding a microphone and looking down at a woman sitting in a rust-colored dress, staring up at him adoringly. It took me a minute to recognize myself. "I'm on the cover of a magazine!" I shrieked.

"A little credit?" he laughed. "I'm on there, too."

"Yeah, but you're on magazines all the time," I said. Lately there'd been a couple spreads about his mysterious disappearance from the Hollywood social scene. His absence, the hubbub that followed the weekend in Maryland, and the opening of his new restaurant had all boosted Ryan's star power considerably. After a lot of wrangling, Ryan had even convinced his agent that making Maryland his home base wouldn't mean quitting the movie business, after all, there were plenty of stars who still worked and didn't live in the madness of Los Angeles.

"Open it," Gran said, poking me.

I flipped inside the magazine to find the feature article, and there, at the top right of the center spread, was a photo of Ryan and me, locked in an embrace and kissing. The article was titled, "Ryan McDonnell finds love with Juliet Manchester's Little Sister." They actually did use my name later in the piece, but the focus was on Ryan's "regular girl" and how his life was changing to accommodate her. It was a good piece, actually, and included some beautiful shots of the house and river, and a few of the party. Gran was even in the article.

In a little box at the bottom of the page was a picture of Juliet, looking beautiful as always. The headline read,

"Stronger on Her Own: Why Juliet Manchester Doesn't Need a Man." The piece talked about Juliet's next projects and only mentioned her divorce briefly.

I grabbed my phone and called her once we'd all read the articles. "What do you think?"

"I think you look amazing in this picture," she said. "You're so photogenic. You could be an actress if you wanted. Want me to make some calls?"

I laughed and looked at Ryan who was listening with Gran and Ronald on speakerphone. "I don't think so," I said. "I'll stick to kayaks. You do the movies."

"I got a new role, actually," she said, sounding excited. "It's not a romcom, Tess. It's a drama, about a woman on her own."

"Perfect," I said, happy at how excited she sounded. "And is Zac leaving you alone?"

There was a brief pause before she said, "No, not at all. But I don't care. He's going to do what he's going to do. That's why I have lawyers."

"Right."

"Good girl," Gran chimed in.

"And guys?" she said, sounding uncertain. "I've got some other news, too…"

We talked for a few more minutes; my heart so full with Juliet's news that I really doubted it could hold any more happiness. I wasn't the only one whose mouth dropped open as she shared the details of the newest developments in her own life—we gaped at one another when she explained what had been going on right under our noses the weekend of Gran's party.

Juliet sounded happy, and once we'd all had a chance to congratulate her, we said goodbye. I closed the magazine and placed the phone on top of it, my own face staring out from its cover.

"I love you guys," I said, a strange calm contentment settling over me, wrapping around me like a comfortable old quilt.

Gran took my hand and Ryan sat next to me on the wicker loveseat. Even Ronald leaned over and dropped a hand on my knee. And we just sat there in the warm Maryland evening, staring out at the water reaching toward Virginia before us and feeling happy. Everything I needed was here, right at my side. Reality and fantasy had blended together, and for once, my life felt perfect.

<<<>>>

WANT to find out what else was happening while Ryan and Tess were falling in love? You can read Juliet's REAL story in HAPPILY EVER HERS!

Juliet Manchester was America's best-loved movie star. But her real life doesn't quite match up to what we see on the screen. When she goes home for a weekend to celebrate her grandmother's birthday, she asks fellow star Ryan McDonnell to pose as her boyfriend to help divert the press from the scandal brewing in her backstory -- **but the farce just may ruin her one chance at something real.**

Jace Morgan was a Marine, and working as a bodyguard to the stars was a great way to make enough money to finish his degree and take care of his mom and brother. But he never planned to develop feelings for his client. And getting involved with Juliet might put everything else in his life in jeopardy.

Can a workplace romance turn into true love? Find out by reserving your copy of HAPPILY EVER HERS today!

ALSO BY DELANCEY STEWART

Want more? Get early releases, sneak peeks and freebies! Join my mailing list here and get a free Mr. Match prequel novella!

The Movie Stars in Maryland Duet:

Book One: Happily Ever His

Book Two: Happily Ever Hers

The MR. MATCH Series:

Book One: Scoring the Keeper's Sister

Book Two: Scoring a Fake Fiancée

Book Three: Scoring a Prince

Book Four: Scoring with the Boss

The LOVE IN THE VINES Series:

Vintage

Redemption Red

Beyond Redemption

A Holiday Delay

The Love in the Vines Box Set (Books 1-4)

The STARR RANCH WINERY Series:

Chasing a Starr

THE GIRLFRIENDS OF GOTHAM Series:

Men and Martinis

Highballs in the Hamptons

Cosmos and Commitment
The Girlfriends of Gotham Box Set

STANDALONES:
Without Words
Without Promises
Mr. Big
Adagio

The PROHIBITED! Duet:
Prohibited!
The Glittering Life of Evie Mckenzie

Made in the USA
Monee, IL
26 August 2019